GEORGES SIMENON
THE FLEMISH HOUSE

Translated by Shaun Whiteside

Georges Simenon (1903–1989) was born in Liège, Belgium. An intrepid traveler with a profound interest in people, Simenon strove on and off the page to understand—and not to judge—the human condition in all its shades. His books include the Inspector Maigret series and a richly varied body of wider work united by its evocative power, its economy of means, and its penetrating psychological insight. He is among the most widely read writers in the global canon.

Shaun Whiteside is a Northern Irish translator of French, Dutch, German, and Italian literature. He has translated many works of nonfiction and novels, including *Manituana* and *Altai*, by Wu Ming; *The Weekend*, by Bernhard Schlink; *Serotonin*, by Michel Houellebecq; and *Magdalena the Sinner*, by Lilian Faschinger, which won the Schlegel-Tieck Prize for German translation in 1997.

THE INSPECTOR MAIGRET BOOKS BY GEORGES SIMENON

Pietr the Latvian
The Late Monsieur Gallet
The Hanged Man of Saint-Pholien
The Carter of La Providence
The Yellow Dog
The Night at the Crossroads
A Crime in Holland
The Grand Banks Café
A Man's Head
The Dancer at the Gai-Moulin
The Two-Penny Bar
The Shadow Puppet
The Saint-Fiacre Affair
The Flemish House
The Madman of Bergerac
The Misty Harbor
Liberty Bar
Lock No. 1
Maigret
Cécile Is Dead
The Cellars of the Majestic
The Judge's House
Signed, Picpus
Inspector Cadaver
Félicie
Maigret Gets Angry
Maigret in New York
Maigret's Holiday
Maigret's Dead Man
Maigret's First Case
My Friend Maigret
Maigret at the Coroner's
Maigret and the Old Lady
Madame Maigret's Friend
Maigret's Memoirs
Maigret at Picratt's
Maigret Takes a Room
Maigret and the Tall Woman
Maigret, Lognon, and the Gangsters
Maigret's Revolver
Maigret and the Man on the Bench
Maigret Is Afraid
Maigret's Mistake
Maigret Goes to School
Maigret and the Dead Girl
Maigret and the Minister
Maigret and the Headless Corpse
Maigret Sets a Trap
Maigret's Failure
Maigret Enjoys Himself
Maigret Travels
Maigret's Doubts
Maigret and the Reluctant Witnesses
Maigret's Secret
Maigret in Court
Maigret and the Old People
Maigret and the Lazy Burglar
Maigret and the Good People of Montparnasse
Maigret and the Saturday Caller
Maigret and the Tramp
Maigret's Anger
Maigret and the Ghost
Maigret Defends Himself
Maigret's Patience
Maigret and the Nahour Case
Maigret's Pickpocket
Maigret Hesitates
Maigret in Vichy
Maigret's Childhood Friend
Maigret and the Killer
Maigret and the Wine Merchant
Maigret's Madwoman
Maigret and the Loner
Maigret and the Informer
Maigret and Monsieur Charles
A Maigret Christmas and Other Stories
Death Threats and Other Stories
The New Investigations of Inspector Maigret

PRAISE FOR GEORGES SIMENON

"A truly wonderful writer . . . Lucid, simple, absolutely in tune with the world he creates." —Muriel Spark

"He's a great writer of detail, of atmosphere. His descriptions of Paris influenced me." —Leïla Slimani

"He is unique and I do not mean just in our times, but in any times." —Henry Miller

"I love reading Simenon. He makes me think of Chekhov." —William Faulkner

"An incredibly expert, dry, and inventive storyteller; the spell is infallible." —V. S. Pritchett

"I've read a lot of Simenon, who's a favorite writer of mine." —Sigrid Nunez

"I want to know what goes on in people's minds. I suppose that's why I love Georges Simenon so much. He was such a master of the small domestic situation." —Ruth Rendell

"Elegant, simple prose . . . as pure as running water." —Roger Ebert

"I really loved the Maigret books by Georges Simenon. He had a real sense of place." —Louise Penny

"Simenon is a master of the quick stroke, the spare narrative." —Larry McMurtry

"Feels incredibly modern . . . A great writer." —Ian Rankin

"The greatest of all, the most genuine novelist we have had in literature." —André Gide

"One of the most important writers of our century."
—Gabriel García Márquez

"Simenon has concentrated noir into a darkness as solid and heavy as the interior of a dwarf star."
—William T. Vollmann

"Simenon's genius . . . was for locating the criminal within every human being . . . Every one of his books is a dark mirror."
—Lucy Sante

"I would do anything for Simenon . . . We love each other with the skin of our souls, heart to heart . . . The novelist of complexes, malaises, mystery, of sticky and sinister souls, and the prince of friendship without shadow or stain."
—Jean Cocteau

"I am a fervent admirer of Simenon . . . He was a maestro."
—Henning Mankell

THE FLEMISH HOUSE

THE FLEMISH HOUSE

GEORGES SIMENON

Translated from the French by Shaun Whiteside

PICADOR

FARRAR, STRAUS AND GIROUX • NEW YORK

Picador
120 Broadway, New York 10271

EU Representative: Macmillan Publishers Ireland Ltd, 1st Floor, The Liffey Trust Centre,
117–126 Sheriff Street Upper, Dublin 1, D01 YC43

Copyright © 1932 by Georges Simenon Limited
Translation copyright © 2014 by Shaun Whiteside
Translation of chapter from *The Madman of Bergerac* copyright © 2015 by Ros Schwartz
GEORGES SIMENON and the Simenon illustration and signature ® **Simenon.tm**®
MAIGRET ® Georges Simenon Limited
All rights reserved
Printed in the United States of America
Originally published in French in 1932 by Fayard, France, as *Chez les Flamands*
English translation first published in 2014 by Penguin Books, Great Britain
English translation published in the United States by Picador
First American edition, 2025

Illustration on page vi by Maria Picassó i Piquer.

Library of Congress Control Number: 2025944727
Paperback ISBN: 978-1-250-39811-6

The publisher of this book does not authorize the use or reproduction
of any part of this book in any manner for the purpose of training artificial intelligence
technologies or systems. The publisher of this book expressly reserves this book
from the Text and Data Mining exception in accordance with Article 4(3) of
the European Union Digital Single Market Directive 2019/790.

Our books may be purchased in bulk for specialty retail/wholesale,
literacy, corporate/premium, educational, and subscription box use. Please contact
MacmillanSpecialMarkets@macmillan.com.

Picador® is a US registered trademark and is used by Macmillan Publishing Group, LLC,
under license from Pan Books Limited.

picadorusa.com • Follow us on social media at @picador or @picadorusa

10 9 8 7 6 5 4 3 2 1

This is a work of fiction. Names, characters, places, organizations, and incidents
either are products of the author's imagination or are used fictitiously. Any resemblance to
actual events, places, organizations, or persons, living or dead, is entirely coincidental.

Contents

1. Anna Peeters 1
2. The *Étoile Polaire* 15
3. The Midwife 29
4. The Portrait 44
5. Maigret's Evening 55
6. The Hammer 72
7. A Three-Hour Gap 86
8. The Visit to the Ursulines 100
9. Around a Wicker Armchair 114
10. Solveig's Song 128
11. Anna's Ending 142

"Of course, they prefer that I not see certain things. But, above all, that I not tell them about others."

* * *

"Will you say everything?"
"Will you?"
"I will try. If I don't, I'll regret it the rest of my life."

—Georges Simenon, *Peuples qui ont faim*, 1934

THE FLEMISH HOUSE

1. Anna Peeters

When Maigret got off the train at Givet station the first person he saw, right opposite his compartment, was Anna Peeters.

It was as if she had predicted that he would stop at this precise spot on the platform! She didn't seem either surprised or proud of the fact. She was just as he had seen her in Paris, as she must always have been, dressed in a gunmetal suit and black shoes, wearing a hat whose shape or even colour it was impossible to remember afterwards.

Here, in the wind that swept the platform, where only a few passengers were now walking, she looked taller, a little stouter. Her nose was red, and she was holding a handkerchief rolled up in a ball.

'I was sure you would come, inspector . . .'

Was she sure of herself, or sure of him? She didn't smile as she greeted him. She was already asking him questions:

'Do you have any other luggage?'

No! Maigret had only his bellows case, in coarse mellowed leather, and he carried it himself, in spite of its weight.

The only people to leave the train were third-class passengers, who had already disappeared. The girl held out her platform ticket to the ticket collector, who looked at her insistently.

Outside, she went on without fuss:

'At first I thought of getting a room ready for you at home. Then I thought it through. In the end I imagine it's better for you to stay at a hotel. So I've booked the best room at the Hôtel de la Meuse.'

They had walked barely a hundred metres along the little streets of Givet, and already everyone was turning to look at them. Maigret walked heavily, dragging his suitcase along at his side. He tried to notice everything: the people, the houses, and particularly his companion.

'What's that noise?' he asked her, hearing a sound that he couldn't identify.

'The Meuse in spate, slapping against the piers of the bridge. Boat transport has been suspended for three weeks now.'

Emerging from a sidestreet, they suddenly came upon the river. It was broad. Its banks were indistinct. In places the brown waters spread into the meadows. Elsewhere, a boathouse emerged from the water.

It held at least a hundred barges, tugs and dredgers, pressed tightly against one another, forming a huge block.

'Here's your hotel. It isn't very cosy. Do you want to stop and take a bath?'

It was baffling! Maigret couldn't define the sensation that he felt. Never, he was sure, had a woman ever aroused his curiosity as much as this one; she stayed calm and unsmiling, made no attempt to look pretty and sometimes dabbed her nose with her handkerchief.

She must have been between twenty-five and thirty. A

lot taller than the average, she was solidly built, with a bone structure that stripped her features of all grace.

The clothes of a lower-middle-class woman, extremely sober. A calm, almost distinguished reserve.

She treated him like a guest. She was at home. She thought of everything.

'I have no reason to take a bath.'

'In that case, will you come straight to the house? Give your suitcase to the porter. Porter! Take this suitcase to room 3. The gentleman will be back shortly.'

And Maigret thought, as he looked at her from the corner of his eye: 'I must look like an idiot!'

For there was nothing of the little boy about him. Even though she wasn't exactly frail, he was twice as wide as she was, and his big overcoat made him look as if he was carved from stone.

'Aren't you tired?'

'Not at all!'

'In that case, I can already tell you the first few bits of information on the way . . .'

She had already given him the first bits of information in Paris! One fine day when he got to his office, he had found this strange woman who had been waiting for him for two or three hours, and whom the office boy had been unable to send away.

'It's personal!' she had announced as he questioned her in front of two police inspectors.

And once they were alone she had handed him a letter. Maigret had recognized the handwriting of one of his wife's cousins, who lived in Nancy.

My dear Maigret,

Miss Anna Peeters has been recommended to me by my brother-in-law, who has known her for about ten years. She is a very responsible young woman, who will tell you of her misfortunes herself. Do what you can for her . . .

'Do you live in Nancy?'

'No, in Givet!'

'But the letter . . .'

'I went to Nancy on purpose, before coming to Paris. I knew my cousin knew someone important in the police force . . .'

She wasn't an ordinary supplicant. She didn't lower her eyes. There was nothing humble about her bearing. She spoke frankly, looking straight ahead, as if to claim what was rightfully hers.

'If you don't agree to look at our case, my parents and I will be lost, and it will be the most hateful miscarriage of justice . . .'

Maigret had taken some notes to sum up her account of things. Quite a muddled family history.

The Peeters family, who owned a grocer's shop on the Belgian border . . . Three children: Anna, who helped them with the business, Maria, who was a teacher, and Joseph, a law student in Nancy . . .

Joseph had had a child by a young local girl . . . The child was three years old . . . But the girl had suddenly disappeared, and the Peeters family were accused of killing or kidnapping her.

Maigret didn't have to get involved in any of that. A

colleague in Nancy was on the case. He had sent him a telegram, and received his categorical reply:

> Peeters family v guilty. Stop. Arrest imminent.

That had made his mind up. He arrived in Givet without a mission, without an official title. And, from the station he fell under the wing of Anna, whom he never grew tired of observing.

The current was violent. The flood formed noisy cascades by each pier of the bridge, and dragged whole trees along.

The wind, which swept through the Meuse valley, blew against the direction of the river, lifting the water to unexpected heights and creating real waves.

It was three in the afternoon. The first hints of night falling.

There were gusts of wind in the almost deserted streets. The few passersby walked quickly, and Anna wasn't the only one blowing her nose.

'See this alleyway on the left . . .'

Anna paused discreetly for a moment, pointing almost imperceptibly at the second house in the sidestreet. A poor-looking, single-storey house. There was already a light on – a paraffin lamp – at one window.

'That's where she lives!'

'Who?'

'Her! Germaine Piedboeuf . . . The girl who . . .'

'The one your brother had a child with?'

'If the child is his! It hasn't even been proved. Look!'

In a doorway a couple could be seen: a hatless girl, probably a little factory worker, and the back of a man who was hugging her.

'Is that her?'

'No, because she's disappeared . . . But she's the same kind of girl . . . You understand? She made my brother believe . . .'

'Doesn't the child look like him?'

She replied crisply:

'He looks like his mother. Come on! These people are always watching from behind their curtains . . .'

'Does she have a family?'

'Her father, who is a night watchman at the factory, and her brother Gérard . . .'

The little house, and particularly the window lit by the paraffin lamp, were now etched in the inspector's memory.

'Do you know Givet?'

'I once passed through without stopping.'

An endless quay, very wide, with mooring posts every twenty metres for the barges. Some warehouses. A low building with a flag flying on it.

'French customs . . . Our house is further away, near Belgian customs . . .'

The water was lapping so furiously that the barges were bumping against one another. Untethered horses were grazing the sparse grass.

'You see that light? That's where we live.'

A customs officer watched them passing without a word. In a group of sailors, someone started speaking Flemish.

'What are they saying?'

She hesitated to reply, and averted her head for the first time.

'That we'll never know the truth!'

And she walked more quickly, against the wind, her back bent to offer less resistance to the wind.

Now they were outside the town. This was the realm of the river, of boats, of customs, of charterers. Here and there an electric light was lit, in the middle of the wind. On a barge, washing flapping on a line. Children playing in the mud.

'Your colleague came to our house again and told us on behalf of the examining magistrate that we were to place ourselves at the disposal of the forces of law and order . . . It's the fourth time everything has been searched, even the water-tank . . .'

They were almost there. The Flemish house was becoming more clearly visible. It was a building of a considerable size, beside the river, in the place where the boats were most concentrated. There was no other house nearby. The only building in sight, a hundred metres away, was the Belgian customs house, flanked by a traffic light.

'If you would care to come in . . .'

On the glass panes of the door there were transparent stickers advertising brass-cleaning creams. A bell rang.

And from the doorway, they were wrapped in warmth, an indefinable atmosphere, quiet and syrupy and dominated by smells. But what were the smells? There was a hint of cinnamon and a darker note of ground coffee.

There was also a smell of paraffin, but with a whiff of genever.

An electric lightbulb, just one. Behind the dark-brown-painted wooden counter a white-haired woman in a black blouse was talking in Flemish to a barge woman. The latter was carrying a child in her arms.

'Please come this way, inspector . . .'

Maigret had had time to see shelves filled with goods. He had particularly noticed, at the end of the counter, the part that had a zinc top, some bottles tipped with tin spouts, containing eau de vie.

He didn't have time to stop. Another glass door, with a curtain. They passed through the kitchen. An old man was sitting in a wicker armchair, right against the stove.

'This way . . .'

A colder corridor. Another door. And it was an unexpected room, half drawing room, half dining room, with a piano, a violin case, a carefully waxed parquet floor, comfortable furniture and reproductions of paintings on the walls.

'Give me your coat.'

The table was laid: a tablecloth with a wide check, silver cutlery and fine china cups.

'You'll have something to drink, won't you?'

Maigret's coat was already in the corridor, and Anna came back in a white silk blouse that made her look even less girlish.

And yet she had a full figure. So why that lack of femininity? It was impossible to imagine her in love. Even harder to imagine a man in love with her.

Everything was prepared in advance. She brought in a steaming coffee pot. She filled three cups. After disappearing again, she came back with a rice tart.

'Sit down, inspector . . . My mother is on her way . . .'

'Are you the pianist?'

'Me and my sister . . . But she has less time than I do. She marks homework in the evening.'

'And the violin?'

'My brother . . .'

'Isn't he in Givet?'

'He'll be here shortly . . . I told him you were coming . . .'

She sliced the tart. She served her guest, without asking him whether he wanted anything. Madame Peeters came in, her hands folded over her stomach, and with a shy smile of welcome on her face, a smile full of melancholy and resignation.

'Anna told me you'd agreed . . .'

She was more Flemish than her daughter and still had a slight accent. But she had very fine features, and her surprisingly white hair gave her a certain nobility. She sat down on the edge of her chair, like a woman who is used to being disturbed.

'You must be hungry, after your journey . . . As for myself, I haven't had an appetite since . . .'

Maigret thought of the old man who was still in the kitchen. Why didn't he come and have some tart as well? At that very moment, Madame Peeters said to her daughter:

'Bring your father a piece . . .'

And, to Maigret:

'He hardly ever leaves his armchair now. He barely knows what's going on.'

Everything about the atmosphere was the opposite of a drama. It was as if the worst events could happen outside, without disturbing the peace and quiet of the Flemish house, in which there was not a speck of dust, not the slightest draught, no sound but the roar of the stove.

And Maigret asked, as he ate the heavy tart:

'What day was it exactly?'

'January the third. A Wednesday.'

'It's the twentieth now . . .'

'Yes, we weren't accused immediately . . .'

'That girl . . . What did you say her name was?'

'Germaine Piedboeuf. She came at about eight o'clock in the evening. She came into the shop, and it was my mother who received her.'

'What did she want?'

Madame Peeters looked as if she was wiping a tear from her eyelid.

'The same as ever. To complain that Joseph never went to see her, never got in touch . . . A boy who works so hard! It's to his credit, I assure you, that he's continuing his studies in spite of everything . . .'

'Did she stay here for long?'

'Perhaps five minutes. I had to tell her not to shout. The sailors could have heard her. Anna came and told her it would be a good idea for her to leave . . .'

'And did she leave?'

'Anna led her outside. I went back into the kitchen and cleared the table.'

'And you haven't seen her again since then?'

'Never!'

'No one around here has met her?'

'They all say they haven't!'

'Did she threaten to commit suicide?'

'No! Women of that kind never kill themselves. More coffee? A piece of cake? Anna made it.'

A new feature to be added to the image of Anna. She was sitting calmly on her chair. She watched the inspector as if their roles had been swapped, as if she belonged to the Quai des Orfèvres, and he to the Flemish house.

'Do you remember what you did that evening?'

It was Anna who replied, with a sad smile.

'We have been asked about this so many times that we've had to remember the tiniest details. After coming home, I went up to my room to get some wool to knit with. When I came down, my sister was at the piano, in this room, and Marguerite had just arrived.'

'Marguerite?'

'Our cousin. The daughter of Dr Van de Weert. They live in Givet. I should tell you straight away, since you'll find out anyway, that she's Joseph's fiancée.'

Madame Peeters got up with a sigh, because the bell had rung in the shop.

She could be heard speaking Flemish, in an almost playful voice, and weighing out beans or peas.

'It was a source of great pain to my mother. It had been decided long since that Joseph and Marguerite would get married. They had got engaged at sixteen. But Joseph had to finish his studies. That was when that child came along.'

'And in spite of that they expected to get married?'

'No! Except that Marguerite didn't want to marry anyone else. They still loved each other.'

'Did Germaine Piedboeuf know that?'

'Yes! But she was counting on getting married! So much so that my brother, to have a bit of peace, had promised he would. The wedding was to be held after his exams.'

And the bell in the shop rang. Madame Peeters tottered through the kitchen.

'I was asking you what happened on the evening of the third.'

'Yes. I was saying that when I came downstairs my sister and Marguerite were in this room. We played the piano until half past ten. My father had gone to bed at nine, as usual. My sister and I walked Marguerite to the bridge.'

'And you didn't meet anyone?'

'No one. It was cold. We came back. The next day we didn't suspect a thing. That afternoon people were saying that Germaine Piedboeuf had disappeared. It was only two days later that people thought of accusing us, because someone had seen her coming in here. The police chief called us in, then your colleague from Nancy. Apparently Monsieur Piedboeuf made a complaint. They searched the house, the cellar, the sheds, everything. They even dug up the garden.'

'Wasn't your brother in Givet on the third?'

'No! He only comes on Saturdays, on his motorbike. Rarely on any other weekday. The whole town is against us, because we are Flemish and have some money.'

A note of pride in her voice. Or rather a superior degree of confidence.

'You can't imagine all the things they made up.'

Again the bell in the shop rang, then the sound of a young voice:

'It's me! Don't disturb yourselves on my account . . .'

Hurried footsteps. A very feminine figure swept into the dining room, stopping abruptly in front of Maigret.

'Oh! Excuse me. I didn't know . . .'

'Inspector Maigret, who's come to help us. My cousin Marguerite.'

A little gloved hand in Maigret's paw. And a nervous smile.

'Anna told me you'd accepted . . .'

She was very elegant, more elegant than pretty. Her face was framed by blonde, slightly wavy hair.

'I gather you were playing the piano.'

'Yes. Music is my only love. Especially when I'm sad . . .'

And she smiled like one of the pretty girls on an advertising calendar. Lips in a pout, a veiled expression, her face leaning slightly forwards . . .

'Maria isn't back?'

'No! Her train must be late.'

The fragile chair creaked when Maigret tried to cross his legs.

'What time did you get here on the third?'

'Half past eight. Perhaps a little earlier. We eat early. My father had friends for bridge.'

'Was the weather the same as today?'

'It was raining. It rained for a whole week.'

'Was the Meuse already in spate?'

'It was starting to be. But the barriers weren't knocked

over until the fifth or the sixth. There were still trains of barges on the water.'

'A piece of cake, inspector? No? A cigar, then?'

Anna held out a box of Belgian cigars and murmured as if in apology:

'It isn't contraband. Part of the house is in Belgium and part in France.'

'So your brother, at least, is completely ruled out because he was in Nancy.'

Anna said stubbornly:

'Not even that! Because of a drunk who claims to have seen him riding his bike along the quay. He said that a fortnight later. As if he could remember! It was Gérard, Germaine Piedboeuf's brother, who found him. There's not much to do around here. So he spends his time looking for witnesses. Just think, they want to bring a civil case and claim 300,000 francs.'

'Where's the child?'

Madame Peeters could be heard hurrying into the shop, where the bell had rung. Anna put the cake on the side table and set the coffee pot down on the stove.

'Their house!'

And the voice of a sailor ordering some genever burst from behind the partition wall.

2. *The* Étoile Polaire

Marguerite Van de Weert rummaged feverishly in her handbag, in a hurry to show them something.

'Haven't you had the *Écho de Givet* yet?'

And she handed Anna a newspaper cutting. She had a modest smile on her lips. Anna passed the paper to Maigret.

'Who gave you the idea?'

'It was me, yesterday, by chance.'

It was only a small advertisement.

> Would the motorcyclist who passed along the Route de Meuse on the evening of 3 January please make himself known. Large reward. Please come to Peeters grocery.

'I didn't dare to give my address, but . . .'

It seemed to Maigret that Anna was looking at her cousin with a hint of impatience as she murmured:

'It's an idea. But no one will come.'

And there was Marguerite, waiting so excitedly to be congratulated!

'Why wouldn't he come? If a motorbike passed along the quay, there's no reason why he wouldn't, since it wasn't Joseph . . .'

The doors were open. Water was starting to sing in the

kettle in the kitchen. Madame Peeters was laying the table for dinner. The sound of voices came from the shop doorway, and suddenly the two girls pricked up their ears.

'Please come in. I have nothing to say to you, but . . .'

'Joseph!' Marguerite stammered, rising to her feet.

There was ardour rather than love in her voice. She was transfigured by it. She didn't dare to sit down again. She waited breathlessly, so much so that one would have imagined that a kind of superman was about to appear.

Now the voice rose in the kitchen.

'Hello, Mother.'

And another voice, one that Maigret didn't know:

'Forgive me, madame, I have some things to check, and I took advantage of the fact that your son was coming here . . .'

At last the two men appeared in the dining room. Joseph Peeters frowned slightly, murmuring with embarrassing sweetness:

'Hello, Marguerite . . .'

She took his hand between both of hers.

'Not too tired, Joseph? Good spirits?'

But Anna, who was calmer, addressed the second person, and pointed to Maigret.

'Detective Chief Inspector Maigret, whom you must know . . .'

'Inspector Machère,' said the other man, extending a hand. 'Is it true that you . . . ?'

But they couldn't talk like that, all standing between the door and the table, which was still laid.

'I'm here in a purely unofficial capacity,' muttered Maigret. 'Just pretend I'm not here . . .'

Someone touched his arm.

'My brother Joseph. Detective Chief Inspector Maigret.'

And Joseph held out a long, cold, bony hand. He was half a head taller than Maigret, and Maigret was over six feet tall. But he was so thin that it looked as if he hadn't stopped growing, even though he was twenty-five.

A nose with pinched nostrils. Tired eyes with heavy dark circles. Short fair hair. He must have had poor eyesight, because his eyelids fluttered constantly as if to escape the light from the lamp.

'Delighted to meet you, inspector. I'm confused.'

He wasn't elegant, however. He took off a greasy raincoat, beneath which he was wearing a suit of neutral grey, of unremarkable cut.

'I met him near the bridge,' said Inspector Machère, 'and I asked him to bring me here behind his motorbike.'

He then turned towards Anna. He addressed her now, as if she were the real mistress of the house. There was no sign of Madame Peeters, or her husband, slumped in the wicker armchair in the kitchen.

'I imagine it's easy to get to the roof?'

Everyone looked at each other.

'Through the skylight in the attic!' Anna replied. 'Do you want to . . .'

'Yes! I want to take a look from up there.'

For Maigret it was an opportunity to take a look around the house.

The staircase was painted and covered so neatly with waxed linoleum that you had to take care not to slip.

On the first floor, a landing with doors leading to three rooms. Joseph and Marguerite had stayed downstairs. Anna walked ahead, and Maigret noticed that she was rolling her hips slightly.

'I'll need to talk to you!' he murmured.

'In a minute!'

They reached the second floor. On one side a garret room, turned into a bedroom, but unoccupied. On the other a huge attic with exposed beams, piled up with cases and bags of merchandise. To reach the skylight, Machère had to climb on two cases.

'Is there no light?'

'I have my torch . . .'

He was a young man with a round, jovial, tirelessly mobile face. Maigret didn't climb on to the roof but looked through the skylight. The wind was blowing in gusts. The roar of the river reached them, and its stormy surface appeared dotted with the light from the occasional gas lamp.

On the left, on the roof cornice, there was a zinc water-tank, at least two cubic metres, towards which the policeman made his way immediately. It must have been designed to capture rain water.

Machère leaned forwards, looked disappointed, walked around on the roof for a few moments and bent to pick something up.

Anna waited in silence, in the darkness, behind Maigret. The inspector's legs appeared again, then his torso, and at last his face.

'A hiding place I only thought of this afternoon, noticing that the people in my hotel only drink rain water . . . But the corpse isn't there.'

'What was the thing you picked up?'

'A handkerchief . . . A woman's handkerchief . . .'

He unfolded it, lit it with his lamp and looked in vain for an initial. The dirty handkerchief had been exposed to the weather for a long time.

'We'll look at that later!' the inspector sighed, walking towards the door.

When they stepped back into the warm atmosphere of the dining room, Joseph Peeters was sitting on the piano stool, reading the advertisement that Marguerite had just shown him. She was standing in front of him, and her wide-brimmed hat and her coat decorated with little flounces emphasized everything diaphanous about her.

'Would you come and see me at the hotel this evening?' Maigret said to the young man.

'Which hotel?'

'The Hôtel de la Meuse!' Anna broke in. 'Are you leaving us already, inspector? I would have invited you to dinner, but . . .'

Maigret walked through the kitchen. Madame Peeters looked at him with astonishment.

'Are you leaving?'

The old man's eyes were empty. He was smoking a meerschaum pipe, without thinking of anything else. He didn't even say goodbye.

Outside there was the wind, the sound of the swollen flood of the Meuse, and the bumps of the boats moored side by side. Inspector Machère hurried to switch places, because he had been standing on Maigret's right.

'Do you think they're innocent?'

'I don't know. Do you have any tobacco?'

'Only some shag . . . People in Nancy talk about you a lot, you know. And that's what worries me. Because these Peeters people . . .'

Maigret had stopped by the boats, and let his eye drift over them. Givet, thanks to the floods which had interrupted boat traffic, looked like a big port. There were several Rhine barges, thousand-tonners, all in black steel. The wooden barges from the north looked like painted toys in comparison.

'I'll have to buy myself a cap!' muttered the inspector, who had to hold on to his bowler hat.

'What did they tell you? That they're innocent, of course!'

They had to speak very loudly, because of the noise of the wind. Givet, 500 metres away, was only a cluster of lights. The Flemish house stood out beneath the stormy sky, its windows lit with a dim yellow glow.

'Where do they come from?'

'From northern Belgium. Old Peeters came from above Limbourg, on the Dutch border. He's twenty years older than his wife, which puts him in his eighties now. He was a basket-maker. A few years ago he still practised his trade with four workmen in the studio behind the house. Now he's totally gaga . . .'

'Are they rich?'

'They're said to be! They own the house. They even lent money to some poor sailors who wanted to buy a boat. You see, sir, they don't have the same mentality as us. Old Peeters has hundreds of thousands of francs, which means he can easily stand his customers a round, as they say. Except that his son's going to be a lawyer. His eldest daughter learned the piano. The other teaches at a famous convent school in Namur. She's quite a senior teacher.'

And Machère pointed to the barges.

'Half the people in there are Flemish. People who don't like changing their habits. Others go to the French bistros near the bridge, drink wine and aperitifs . . . The Flemish want their genever, someone who understands their language, and everything . . . Each boat buys provisions for a week or more . . . And I'm not talking about contraband! They're in the right place for that . . .'

Their overcoats stuck to their bodies. The water was lapping so violently that it splashed over the decks of the laden barges.

'They don't think the same way as we do. For them, it's not a bistro. It's a grocery, even though they serve drinks at the counter. And even the women have a drop when they're doing their shopping. Apparently that's what brings in the most . . .'

'The Piedboeufs?' asked Maigret.

'Little people. A factory security man. The daughter was a secretary in the same company. The son still works there.'

'A sensible boy?'

'I wouldn't say that. He doesn't do a lot of work. He prefers playing billiards at the Café de la Mairie. He's a good-looking guy and he knows it . . .'

'The daughter?'

'Germaine? She's had some lovers. You know, she's one of those girls you find in dark corners at night, with a man. Which doesn't mean Joseph Peeters isn't the father . . . I've seen the child. It looks like him. What you can't deny, at any rate, is that she went into the house on the third of January, shortly after eight in the evening, and since then no one has seen her again.'

Inspector Machère was speaking frankly.

'I've looked everywhere. I even did a detailed summary of the area with an architect. There was only one thing I'd forgotten: the roof. Normally you wouldn't think of hiding a corpse on a roof. I went up there, just a moment ago. I found a handkerchief, but nothing else . . .'

'And the Meuse?'

'Quite! I was going to talk to you about that . . . You know, don't you, that almost all drowned bodies are found on the barriers . . . There are eight between here and Namur . . . Except that two days after the crime, the river had swollen so much that the barriers were knocked over, as happens every winter . . . Which means that Germaine Piedboeuf could easily have got as far as Holland, if not the sea . . .'

'I was told that Joseph Peeters wasn't here the evening when . . .'

'I know! That's what he claims. A witness saw a motorbike that looked like his. He swears it wasn't him.'

'Doesn't he have an alibi?'

'He does and he doesn't. I went back to Nancy specially. He lives in a furnished room where he can come back without being seen by his landlady. He also frequents the cafés and bars where the students meet every night. No one can remember exactly whether it was on the third, the fourth or the fifth that he spent the night in one of those bars . . .'

'Might Germaine Piedboeuf have killed herself?'

'She wasn't that sort of woman. A little person with poor health and less than perfect morals, but who loved her son . . .'

'Someone else might have attacked her . . .'

This time Machère said nothing and let his eye drift across the boats that formed a little island a few metres away from the shore.

'I thought of that. I investigated all the sailors. Most of them are responsible people who live on board with their families and children. The only one that made me pause was the *Étoile Polaire*. The last boat upstream . . . The dirtiest one, which looks as if it's about to sink . . .'

'What is it?'

'A boat skippered by a Belgian from Tilleur, near Liège . . . An old brute who has been investigated twice for indecent assault . . . The boat hasn't been maintained . . . No one will insure it . . . There were lots of stories about women and little girls . . . But why do you want to . . . ?'

The two men walked towards the bridge again. As they got closer, they entered the light of the town's street lamps.

On their right they saw bistros, French bistros, where mechanical pianos held sway.

'I'm having him watched . . . All the same, there's the witness statement about the motorbike . . .'

'Which hotel are you staying at?'

'The Hôtel de la Gare . . .'

Maigret held out his hand.

'I will see you again, old man . . . Of course, you're the one leading the inquiry . . . I'm only here as an amateur . . .'

'What do you want me to do? If they don't find the body, there's no proof . . . And if it's been thrown in the water, we'll never find it . . .'

Maigret distractedly shook his hand, and as they reached the bridge he went inside the Hôtel de la Meuse.

As he ate his dinner, Maigret had jotted in his notebook:

> Opinions about the Peeters family.
> MACHÈRE – They don't see themselves as a bistro.
> THE HOTELIER – They consider themselves a cut above. Would I have my son train as a lawyer, for example?
> A SAILOR – In Flanders they're all like that!
> SOMEONE ELSE – They stick together like freemasons!

And it was curious, from the town, from the bridge that constituted the central point of Givet, to look across at the Flemish side. It looked like a French town. Little streets. Cafés filled with people playing billiards or dominoes. The smell of pastis and general familiarity.

Then that stretch of river. The customs building. And

last of all, right at the end, on the edge of the countryside, the Flemish house: the grocery crammed to the rafters with goods; the little zinc bar for the genever-drinkers; the kitchen and that senile old husband in his wicker armchair up against the stove; the dining room and the piano, the violin, the comfortable seats, the home-made tart, Anna and Marguerite, the checked tablecloth. Joseph, long, thin and sickly, arriving on his motorbike to an atmosphere of general admiration!

The Hôtel de la Meuse was a hotel for commercial travellers. The landlord knew everyone. They each had their towel.

Joseph Peeters came in as a stranger, shyly, at about nine o'clock, swooped towards the inspector and stammered:

'Any news?'

However, everyone was looking at them, and Maigret preferred to take the man to his room.

'What is it?'

'Do you know about the advertisement? . . . A motorcyclist has turned up . . . A car mechanic from Dinant, who drove by that evening, at about half past eight, right opposite the house . . .'

Maigret's suitcase hadn't yet been opened. The inspector was sitting on the side of the bed, leaving the only armchair for his visitor.

'Do you really love Marguerite?'

'Yes . . . that is . . .'

'That is . . . ?'

'She's my cousin! I wanted to make her my wife . . . It was decided a long time ago . . .'

'You still had a child with Germaine Piedboeuf!'

A silence. Then, with a slight stammer, a faint:

'Yes . . .'

'Did you love her?'

'I don't know!'

'Would you have married her?'

'I don't know . . .'

Maigret saw in the glare of the light, with his thin face, his tired eyes, his weary features, Joseph Peeters didn't dare to look him in the eye.

'How did it happen?'

'We were going out, Germaine and I . . .'

'And Marguerite?'

'No! That was different . . .'

'So?'

'She told me she was going to have a child . . . I didn't know what to do . . .'

'It was your mother who . . .'

'My mother and my sisters . . . They proved to me that I wasn't the first, that Germaine had had . . .'

'Affairs?'

The window looked out on to the river, at the very spot where it broke against the piers of the bridge. And it was a constant, loud roar.

'Do you love Marguerite?'

The young man got up, worried and uneasy.

'What do you mean?'

'Do you love Marguerite or Germaine?'

'I . . . That is . . .'

He had beads of sweat on his forehead.

'How do you expect me to know? . . . My mother's already fixed me up with a legal office in Reims . . .'

'You and Marguerite?'

'I don't know . . . I met the other one at a dance . . .'

'Germaine?'

'At a ball I'd been forbidden to go to . . . I drove her home . . . On the way . . .'

'And Marguerite?'

'It's not the same thing . . . I . . .'

'You didn't leave Nancy on the night of the third to the fourth?'

Maigret had heard enough. He walked towards the door. He had got the measure of his man: a tall, bony boy, but with a soft character, whose pride was sustained by the admiration of his sisters and his cousin.

'What have you been doing since then?'

'Studying for my exam . . . It's the last one . . . Anna sent me a telegram to come and see you . . . Did you . . .'

'No! I have no further need of you! You can go back to Nancy.'

A face that Maigret would not forget: big, clear eyes, lined red with worry. A waistcoat that was too tight. Trousers with pockets on the knees.

In the same clothes, adding only a raincoat, Joseph Peeters would go back to Nancy, on his motorbike, without exceeding the speed limit . . .

A little student's bedsit, in the home of some poor old lady . . . Classes that he must never miss . . . The café at lunchtime . . . Billiards in the evening . . .

'If it was useful to me to see you, I would let you know!'

And Maigret, on his own now, leaned on the window-sill, receiving the wind from the valley, seeing the Meuse hurrying towards the plain, seeing in the distance a small, veiled light: the Flemish house.

In the shadow, a jumbled collection of boats, masts, funnels, the rounded sterns of barges.

The *Étoile Polaire* at its head.

He went outside, filling his pipe, turning up the collar of his overcoat, and the wind was so strong that in spite of his bulk he had to brace himself to stand up to it.

3. The Midwife

As usual, Maigret had got up at eight o'clock in the morning. With his hands in the pockets of his overcoat, his pipe between his teeth, he stood motionless facing the bridge for a long while, now watching the river in its madness, now letting his gaze drift over the passersby.

The wind was as violent as it had been the previous day. It was much colder than in Paris.

But how exactly could you tell that you were at the border? Was it the transition to Belgian-style houses with their ugly brown brickwork, their freestone doorsteps and their windows decorated with copper pots?

The harder, more chiselled features of the Walloons? The khaki uniforms of the Belgian customs officers? Or was it that the currency of both countries was used in the shops?

In any case, it was unmistakable: you were at the border. Two peoples lived side by side.

Maigret felt better than ever as he stepped into a waterside bistro for a hot rum. A French bistro, with the whole range of multicoloured aperitifs. Mirrors on pale walls. And people standing drinking their morning glass of white wine.

There were about ten sailors around the owners of two tugs. They were talking about the possibility of going down the river in spite of everything.

'There's no chance of getting beyond the Dinant bridge! Even if you could, we'd be forced to take fifteen French francs per ton. It's too expensive. At that price it's better to wait.'

And they looked at Maigret. One man nudged another with his elbow. The inspector had been spotted.

'There's a Fleming who's talking about leaving tomorrow, without an engine, and just letting himself be carried along by the current . . .'

There were no Flemings in the café. They preferred the Peeters' shop, all in dark wood, with its smells of coffee, chicory, cinnamon and genever. They must have stayed there with their elbows on the counter for hours at a time, stretching out an idle conversation, looking with their pale eyes at the stickers on the door.

Maigret listened to what was being said around him. He learned that the Flemish sailors were not liked, not so much personally, but because, with their boats and their powerful engines, maintained like kitchen utensils, they were in competition with the French and accepted freight at derisory prices.

'And what if they're involved in killing girls?'

They were speaking for Maigret's benefit, looking at him out of the corners of their eyes.

'I wonder what's keeping the police from arresting the Peeters family! Maybe they've got too much money so they're in two minds about it . . .'

Maigret left the bistro and wandered along the quayside for another few minutes, looking at the brown water, which was sweeping tree branches along. In the little street on the left he spotted the house that Anna had pointed out to him.

The light that morning was sad, the sky a uniform grey. The people, who were cold, didn't linger in the streets.

The inspector walked to the door and pulled on the bell cord. It was just after a quarter past eight. The woman who opened the door must have been busy with some big cleaning project, because she wiped her hands on her wet apron.

'Who do you want?'

At the end of the corridor a kitchen could be seen, with a bucket and a brush in the middle of it.

'Is Monsieur Piedboeuf at home?'

She looked him suspiciously up and down.

'The father or the son?'

'The father.'

'I suppose you're from the police? Then you should know that at this time of day he's in bed, given that he's a night watchman and never comes home before seven in the morning . . . Now, if you'd like to go upstairs . . .'

'There's no point. And the son?'

'He left for the office ten minutes ago.'

The sound of a spoon falling came from the kitchen. Maigret saw a bit of a child's head.

'That wouldn't by any chance be . . .' he began.

'It's the son of poor Mademoiselle Germaine, yes! Come in or go out! You're freezing the whole house . . .'

The inspector came in. The walls of the corridor were painted to look like marble. The kitchen was in chaos, and the woman muttered vaguely as she picked up her brush and bucket.

On the table there were dirty cups and plates. A two-and-a-half-year-old boy was sitting all by himself, eating a boiled egg, clumsily, smearing himself with yolk.

The woman must have been about forty. She was thin, with an ascetic face.

'Are you bringing him up?'

'Since they killed his mother, I've been looking after him most of the time, yes! His grandfather has to sleep half the day. There's no one else in the house. And when I have clients to go and see, I have to leave him with a neighbour.'

'Clients?'

'I'm a qualified midwife.'

She had taken off her checked apron, as if it stripped her of her dignity.

'Don't be scared, my little Jojo!' she said to the child, who was looking at the visitor and had stopped eating.

Did he look like Joseph Peeters? It was hard to say. At any rate, he was a feeble child. His features were irregular, his head was too big, his neck was thin, and above all he had a thin, wide mouth that looked as if it belonged to a child of at least ten.

He didn't take his eyes off Maigret but he didn't say anything. He didn't express any more emotion when the midwife felt the need to kiss him, in what was perhaps a rather theatrical way, exclaiming:

'The poor love! Eat your egg, my darling!'

She hadn't invited Maigret to sit down. There was water on the floor and a soup cooking on the stove.

'So it must have been you they went to fetch from Paris?'

The voice was not quite aggressive, but it was far from amiable.

'What do you mean?'

'There's no point being mysterious here! We know everything!'

'Explain yourself.'

'Because you know as well as I do! A nice job you've accepted here! . . . But aren't the police always on the side of the rich?'

Maigret had frowned, not because of the gratuitous accusation, but because of what the midwife's words revealed.

'It was the Flemings themselves who told everyone that we might worry them for now, but that it wouldn't last, and that things would change when some sort of detective chief inspector arrived from Paris!'

She smiled meanly.

'My goodness! We gave them plenty of time to prepare their lies! They know very well that the body of Mademoiselle Germaine will never be found! Eat, my little one. Don't fret . . .'

And tears came to her eyes as she looked at the boy holding his spoon in the air, without taking his eyes off Maigret.

'Do you have anything in particular to tell me?' the inspector asked her.

'Nothing at all! The Peeters must have given you all the information you wanted, and they must even have told you that the child isn't their Joseph's!'

Was it worth pressing the point? Maigret was the enemy. There was a feeling of hate floating in the air of this poor house.

'Now, if you want to see Monsieur Piedboeuf, you only need to come back at about midday . . . That's when he gets up and Monsieur Gérard comes back from the office . . .'

She led him back along the corridor and closed the door behind him. The first-floor shutters were down.

Maigret found Inspector Machère near the Flemish house, in conversation with two sailors, whom he left as he spotted Maigret.

'What are they saying?'

'I was talking to them about the *Étoile Polaire* . . . They think they remember that on the third of January the owner left the Café des Mariniers at about eight o'clock, and that he was drunk, as he was every evening . . . At this time of day he's still asleep . . . I've just been on his boat, and he didn't even hear me . . .'

Behind the windows of the grocery shop the white head of Madame Peeters could be seen, observing the policemen.

The conversation was disjointed. The two men looked around without examining anything in particular.

On one side, the river with the overturned barriers, dragging flotsam along at a speed of nine kilometres an hour.

On the other, the house.

'There are two entrances!' said Machère. 'The one we

can see, and another one, behind the building . . . In the courtyard there's a well . . .'

He hastened to add:

'I've searched it . . . I think I've searched everything . . . And yet, I don't know why, I have a sense that the corpse wasn't thrown into the Meuse . . . What was that woman's handkerchief doing on the roof?'

'You know they've found the motorcyclist?'

'I heard. But that doesn't prove that Joseph Peeters wasn't here that evening.'

Of course! There was no proof either for or against! There wasn't even any serious evidence!

Germaine Piedboeuf had come into the shop at about eight o'clock. The Flemings claimed she had gone out again a few minutes later, but no one else had seen her.

That was all!

The Piedboeufs had levelled accusations and were demanding 300,000 francs in damages.

Two boatmen's wives came into the grocery, and the bell rang.

'Do you still believe, sir . . .'

'I don't believe anything at all, old man! See you later . . .'

He went into the shop in turn. The two customers shifted up to make room for him. Madame Peeters called out:

'Anna!'

And she came hurrying, opening the glass kitchen door.

'Come in, inspector . . . Anna will be here very shortly . . . She's tidying the bedrooms . . .'

She turned her attention back to her customers, and Maigret, crossing the kitchen, turned into the corridor and slowly climbed the stairs. Anna mustn't have heard. There were noises coming from a room whose door was open, and Maigret suddenly saw the girl, with a handkerchief knotted around her head, busy brushing a pair of men's trousers.

She saw the visitor in the mirror, turned swiftly and dropped the brush.

'How long have you been there?'

She seemed much the same, although casually dressed for the morning. She still had the air of a well-brought-up, slightly distant girl.

'Excuse me . . . I was told you were upstairs . . . Is this your brother's room?'

'Yes . . . He left first thing this morning . . . The exam is very hard . . . He wants to pass it with the best possible distinction, like the other ones . . .'

On a sideboard there was a big portrait of Marguerite Van de Weert, in a light-coloured dress, wearing an Italian straw hat.

And the girl had written, in long, pointed handwriting, the beginning of 'Solveig's Song':

Winter may pass
Beloved spring
May pass . . .

Maigret was holding the portrait. Anna looked at him insistently, even with a hint of suspicion, as if she feared a smile.

'Those are lines from Ibsen,' she said.
'I know . . .'
And Maigret recited the end of the poem:

I wait for you here,
O my handsome betrothed,
Until my very last day . . .

He nearly smiled, however, because he was looking at the trousers that Anna was still holding.

It was unexpected, ridiculous or moving, those heroic lines in the dark setting of a student's room.

Joseph Peeters, long and thin, badly dressed, with his fair hair that no cream could tame, his disproportionately large nose, his short-sighted eyes . . .

O my handsome betrothed . . .

And that portrait of a provincial girl, diaphanously pretty!

It wasn't the prestigious context of Ibsen's play. She wasn't proclaiming her faith to the stars! Like a good middle-class girl she copied out some lines at the bottom of a portrait.

I wait for you here . . .

And she really had waited! In spite of Germaine Piedboeuf! In spite of the child! In spite of the years!

Maigret felt vaguely awkward. He looked at the table covered with a green blotting pad, with a brass inkwell that must have been a present, and a Galalith pen holder.

Mechanically, he opened one of the drawers of the sidetable and saw, in a cardboard box without a lid, some amateur photographs.

'My brother has a camera.'

Some young people in students' caps . . . Joseph on his motorbike, his hand on the throttle lever ready for a fast start . . . Anna at the piano . . . Another girl, thinner and sadder . . .

'That's my sister Maria.'

And suddenly there was a little passport photograph, as gloomy as all portraits of that kind, because of the brutal contrast of black and white.

A girl, but so frail, so small that she looked like a child. Big eyes took up the whole of her face. She wore a ridiculous hat and seemed to be looking with fear at the camera.

'Germaine, isn't it?'

Her son looked like her.

'Was she sick?'

'She had tuberculosis. She wasn't very healthy.'

Anna was! Tall and well built, she seemed in a perfect mental and physical equilibrium. At last she set the trousers down on the counterpane.

'I've just been to her house . . .'

'What did they say? They must have . . .'

'I only saw a midwife . . . and the little boy . . .'

She didn't ask any questions, as though out of modesty. There was something discreet about her demeanour.

'Is your bedroom next door?'

'Yes . . . My bedroom, which is also my sister's . . .'

There was a connecting door, which Maigret opened. The other room was brighter, because its windows looked out on to the quay. The bed was already made. It wasn't untidy in the slightest, not so much as a piece of clothing on the furniture.

Only two nightdresses neatly folded on the two pillows.

'You're twenty-five?'

'Twenty-six.'

Maigret wanted to ask a question. He didn't know how to do it.

'You've never been engaged?'

'Never.'

But that wasn't entirely what he had wanted to ask. She impressed him, particularly now that he had seen her room. She impressed him as an enigmatic statue might have done. He wondered if her unappealing flesh had ever trembled, if she was anything but a devoted sister, a model daughter, a mistress of the house, a Peeters, if, in the end, beneath that surface, there was a woman!

And she didn't look away. She didn't hide. She must have felt that he was studying her figure as much as her features but she didn't so much as blink.

'We never see anyone apart from our cousins, the Van de Weerts . . .'

Maigret hesitated, and his voice wasn't entirely natural when he said:

'I'm going to ask you to do an experiment for me. Will

you go down to the dining room and play the piano for me until I call you. For as long as possible, the same piece as on the third of January . . . Who was playing?'

'Marguerite. She sings and accompanies herself. She's had singing lessons.'

'Do you remember the piece?'

'It's always the same. "Solveig's Song" . . . But . . . I . . . I don't understand.'

'It's just an experiment . . .'

She left the room backwards, and was about to close the door.

'No! Leave it open.'

A few moments later, some fingers ran carelessly over the keyboard, producing disconnected chords. And Maigret, without wasting any time, opened the cupboards in the girls' bedroom.

The first was the linen cupboard. Regular piles of shirts, trousers and well-ironed skirts . . .

The chords followed on from one another. The tune became recognizable. And Maigret's fat fingers came and went among the white cloth underwear.

An onlooker would probably have taken him for a lover, or even for a man satisfying some hidden passion.

Coarse underwear, solid, hard-wearing, inelegant. The underwear of the two sisters must have been mixed together.

Then it was the turn of a drawer: stockings, suspenders, boxes of hairpins . . . No powder . . . No perfume, except a bottle of Russian eau de Cologne that must only have been used on important occasions.

The sound grew louder... The house was filled with music... And gradually a voice accompanied the piano, and came to the fore.

I wait for you here,
Oh my handsome betrothed...

It wasn't Marguerite who was singing – it was Anna Peeters! She clearly enunciated each syllable, and lingered wistfully on certain phrases.

Maigret's fingers were still working fast, probing around in the fabric.

In a pile of linen there was a rustle that was not of cloth, but of paper.

Another portrait. An amateur portrait, in sepia. A young man with curly hair and fine features, his upper lip jutting forward in a confident and slightly ironic smile.

Maigret didn't know who the man reminded him of. But he reminded him of something.

Until my very last day...

A serious voice, almost a masculine voice fading slowly away. Then a call:

'Should I go on, inspector?'

He closed the doors of the cupboards, put the photograph into his waistcoat pocket and darted into Joseph Peeters' room.

'Don't bother.'

He noticed that Anna was paler when she came back.

Had she been putting too much soul into her singing? Her eyes scoured the room but found nothing unusual.

'I don't understand . . . I would like to ask you something, inspector. You saw Joseph last night . . . What did you think of him? . . . Do you think he's capable . . .'

Probably downstairs, she had taken off the headscarf that covered her head. Maigret even had a sense that she had washed her hands.

'Everyone, you understand, everyone,' she went on, 'must acknowledge his innocence! He has to be happy!'

'With Marguerite Van de Weert?'

She said nothing. She sighed.

'How old is your sister Maria?'

'Twenty-eight . . . Everyone agrees that she's going to be headmistress of the school in Namur.'

Maigret touched the portrait in his pocket.

'No lovers?'

And she replied, straight away:

'Maria?'

It meant, 'Maria, a lover? You don't know her!'

'I'm going to pursue my inquiry!' said Maigret, moving towards the landing.

'Have you had any results so far?'

'I don't know.'

She followed him down the stairs. As they passed through the kitchen, he noticed old Peeters, who had taken up his place in his armchair and plainly couldn't see him.

'He isn't aware of anything any more,' Anna sighed.

In the grocery, there were three or four people. Madame

Peeters was pouring genever into glasses. She greeted him with a slight bow, without setting down her bottle, then went on talking Flemish.

She must have explained that the visitor was the police inspector who had come from Paris, because the sailors turned respectfully towards Maigret.

Outside, Inspector Machère was busy studying a spot of ground where the soil was less firm than elsewhere.

'Anything new?' Maigret asked.

'I don't know! I'm still looking for the corpse. Because until we get our hands on it, it will be impossible to get these people.'

And he turned towards the Meuse as if to say that that wasn't the way the body had gone.

4. The Portrait

It was just after midday. Maigret, perhaps for the fourth time since that morning, was walking along the riverbank. On the other side of the Meuse there was a big whitewashed factory wall, a gate and dozens of workmen and women coming out of it, on foot or by bicycle.

The encounter took place a hundred metres before the bridge. The inspector passed someone, looking at him straight on, and when he turned round he saw the other man turning round as well.

He was the original of the portrait found among Anna's clothes.

A brief hesitation. It was the young man who took a step towards Maigret.

'Are you the policeman from Paris?'

'Gérard Piedboeuf, I presume?'

The policeman from Paris. It was the fifth or sixth time since that morning that Maigret had heard himself referred to in those terms. And he understood the nuance very clearly. His colleague Machère, from Nancy, was there to carry out inquiries, nothing else. They watched him coming and going and when they thought they knew something they ran to tell him.

As for Maigret, he was 'the policeman from Paris',

summoned by the Flemings, who had come specially to wash them of all suspicion. And, in the street, people who knew him already watched after him without the slightest sympathy.

'Have you come from my house?'

'I went there, but early this morning, and I only saw your nephew . . .'

Gérard was no longer quite the same age as he had been in the portrait. If his figure was still very young, and his hair and clothes were young as well, close up it was clear that he had turned twenty-five some time ago.

'Did you want to speak to me?'

In any case, shyness was not one of his faults. He didn't once look away. His eyes were brown and very shining, eyes that women were bound to like, particularly since his complexion was dark and his lips well formed.

'Bah! I've only just begun my inquiries . . .'

'On behalf of the Peeters, I know! The whole town knows! We knew even before you got here. You're a friend of the family and you're going out of your way to . . .'

'I'm doing no such thing! Ah, your father's getting up . . .'

They could see the little house. On the first floor the shutter rose, and they made out the form of a man with a big grey moustache looking through the glass.

'He's seen us!' said Gérard. 'He's going to get dressed . . .'

'Did you know the Peeters personally?'

They walked along the quayside, turning around every time they reached a mooring post a hundred metres from the grocery. The air was sharp. Gérard was wearing an overcoat that was too thin, but whose very slim fit must have appealed to him.

'What do you mean?'

'Your sister has been Joseph Peeters' mistress for three years. Didn't she used to go to his house?'

Gérard shrugged.

'If we go through all that again in detail! First of all, shortly before the child was born, Joseph swore that he would marry her. Then Dr Van de Weert came, on behalf of the Peeters, to offer 10,000 francs for my sister to leave the country and never come back. Germaine's first outing after she had recovered from the birth was to go and show the child to the Peeters. A terrible scene, because they wouldn't let her in, and the old woman treated her as a loose woman . . . In the end things settled down . . . Joseph still promised to get married . . . But first he wanted to finish his studies . . .'

'And what about you?'

'Me?'

He began by pretending not to understand. But almost immediately he changed his mind and assumed a smile that was both vain and ironic.

'Have they told you something?'

Maigret, while walking along the quay, took the little portrait from his pocket and showed it to his companion.

'Good heavens! I had no idea that still existed!'

He tried to take it, but Maigret put it back in his wallet.

'Was she the one who . . . ? No! It's not possible. She's too proud for that. At least she is now!'

And throughout the entire conversation Maigret didn't take his eyes off his companion. Was he tubercular, like his sister and probably like Joseph's son? It wasn't certain! But he had the charm of certain consumptives: fine features, transparent skin, lips that were sensual and mocking at the same time.

His elegance was that of an office clerk, and he had thought it necessary to put a crêpe armband on his beige overcoat.

'Did you woo her?'

'It was a long time ago . . . It goes back to the time when my sister didn't yet have a child. At least four years.'

'Go on.'

'My father's just taken a look at the corner of the street . . .'

'Go on anyway.'

'It was Sunday. Germaine was supposed to be going to visit the Rochefort caves with Joseph Peeters. At the last moment they asked me to go, because one of his sisters was coming along. The caves are twenty-five kilometres from here. We had a picnic. I was in very high spirits. Afterwards the two couples parted to go walking the woods . . .'

Maigret's eyes were still on him, without expressing his thoughts in any way.

'And then?'

'Well? Yes . . .'

And Gérard gave a fatuous, sly smile.

'I couldn't even tell you how it went. I don't tend to drag things out. She didn't expect it and . . .'

Maigret put a hand on his shoulder and asked him slowly:

'Is this true?'

And he knew that it was. Anna, at that moment then, had been twenty-one . . .

'Afterwards?'

'Nothing! She's too ugly. Coming back on the train, she stared into my eyes, and I worked out that the best thing to do was to dump her . . .'

'She didn't try . . . ?'

'Nothing at all! I made sure to avoid her. She felt that there was no point insisting. Except when we pass in the street I have a sense that if looks could kill . . .'

They walked towards Piedboeuf senior, who, without a false collar and with his feet in cloth slippers, was waiting for the two men.

'They tell me you came to see us this morning. Please come in . . . Have you told the inspector, Gérard?'

Maigret went up the narrow staircase, whose white wooden steps didn't look very solid. The same room acted as kitchen, dining room and drawing room. It was poor and ugly. The table was covered by a waxed cloth with a blue pattern.

'Who would have killed her?' said Piedboeuf abruptly; he seemed to be a man of mediocre intelligence. 'She left that evening, telling me that she hadn't had her monthly, or even any news from Joseph.'

'Her monthly?'

'Yes! He paid a hundred francs a month for the care of the child . . . That's the least he could do and . . .'

Gérard, who felt that his father was about to launch off on a familiar jeremiad, interrupted him.

'The inspector isn't interested in that! What he wants are facts, proof! Well, at the very least I have proof that Joseph Peeters, who claims not to have come to Givet that day, was there . . . He came on his motorbike and . . .'

'Are you talking about the witness? It's worthless now. Another motorcyclist has turned up to say he was the one who drove along the quay just after eight o'clock . . .'

'Ah!'

And, aggressively:

'Are you against us?'

'I'm not with anyone! I'm not against anyone! I'm just looking for the truth.'

But Gérard chuckled and said loudly to his father:

'The inspector didn't come here to try and catch us out . . . You'll forgive me, inspector . . . But I need to eat . . . I have to earn a living, and my office opens at two o'clock!'

What was the point of talking? Maigret cast one last glance around him, spotted the child's cot in the next room and headed towards the door.

Machère was waiting for him at the Hôtel de la Meuse. The travelling salesmen were having their lunch in a little room separated from the café by a glass door.

But in the café itself you could have a snack, without a tablecloth, and there were some people eating like that.

Machère wasn't alone. A little man with monstrously wide shoulders and the long arms of a hunchback was having an aperitif at his table, and got up when he saw Maigret coming in.

'The owner of the *Étoile Polaire*!' announced Machère, who was very animated. 'Gustave Cassin . . .'

Maigret sat down. A glance at the saucers told him that his companions were already on their third aperitif.

'Cassin has something to tell you . . .'

That was exactly what the man was waiting for! As soon as Machère fell silent, he started off, leaning importantly on the chief inspector's shoulder:

'You have to say what you have to say, am I right? . . . Except there's no need to say it when people are asking you not to say it . . . As my late father used to say: don't overdo it!'

'A beer!' said Maigret to the approaching waiter.

And he pushed back his bowler hat and unbuttoned his overcoat. Then, as the sailor stumbled for words, he muttered:

'If I'm not mistaken, on the evening of the third of January you were completely drunk . . .'

'Completely, that's not true! . . . I'd had a few glasses, but I was still walking straight . . . And I clearly saw what I saw . . .'

'You saw a motorbike turning up and stopping outside the Flemish house?'

'Me? . . . Never in my life! . . .'

Machère gestured to Maigret not to interrupt the man and encouraged him to continue with a wave of his hand.

'I saw a woman on the quay . . . I'll tell you who it

was . . . The one of the two sisters who's never in the shop and takes the train every day . . .'

'Maria?'

'Maybe that's her name . . . Thin, with blonde hair . . . Well! It wasn't natural for her to be out of doors, given that the wind was rattling the moorings of the boats . . .'

'At what time?'

'When I came back to go to bed . . . Perhaps about eight . . . Perhaps a bit later . . .'

'Did she see you?'

'No! Rather than going on my way, I pressed myself against the customs shed, because I thought she was waiting for a lover, and I was hoping to have a laugh . . .'

'Really! You've been sentenced twice for indecent assault . . .'

Cassin smiled, showing a row of rotten teeth. He was a man of indeterminate age, his hair still brown, low over his forehead, but his face was very wrinkled.

He was very concerned with the effect he produced, and every time he uttered a phrase he looked first at Maigret, then at Inspector Machère, and then at a customer sitting behind him, listening to the conversation.

'Go on!'

'She wasn't waiting for a lover.'

Nonetheless he hesitated. He gulped down the contents of his glass in one, and called out to the waiter:

'Same again!'

And in the next breath:

'She checked that no one was coming . . . During that

time people came out of the grocery, not through the shop but by the back door . . . They were carrying something long and they threw it into the Meuse, just between my boat and *Les Deux Frères*, which is moored behind it . . .'

'How much is that?' Maigret asked the waiter, getting to his feet.

He didn't look surprised. Machère was completely discomfited. As for the sailor, he didn't know what to think.

'Come with me.'

'Where to?'

'Doesn't matter. Come!'

'I'm waiting for the drink I just ordered . . .'

Maigret waited patiently. He told the landlord that he would come for lunch a few minutes later, and led the drunk towards the quay.

It was the time of day when the place was deserted, because everyone was eating. Big drops of rain started falling.

'Where exactly were you?' Maigret asked.

He knew the customs building. He saw Cassin pressing himself into a corner.

'You didn't move from there?'

'Definitely not! I didn't want to get involved!'

'Let me take your place!'

He stayed there only for a few seconds and then said, looking straight at the man:

'You'll have to find something else, my friend!'

'What do you mean, something else?'

'I'm saying that your story doesn't hold water. From here you can't see the grocery, or the stretch of river bounded by the two boats.'

'When I say it was here, what I mean is . . .'

'No! That's enough! I'm telling you again, find something else! Come and see me when you've found it. And if it isn't good enough, well, it might be necessary to bang you up again . . .'

Machère couldn't believe his ears. Embarrassed by his failure, he in turn had pressed himself against the wall, and was checking Maigret's claims.

'Obviously! . . .' he grunted.

The sailor didn't even try to reply. He had lowered his head. An ironic, mean glance was fixed on Maigret's feet.

'Don't forget what I just told you: a different, more plausible story . . . Otherwise, prison! . . . Come, Machère . . .'

And Maigret turned on his heels and headed towards the bridge, filling his pipe.

'Do you think that that sailor . . .'

'I think that this evening or tomorrow he'll come and bring us more evidence of the Peeters' guilt.'

Inspector Machère was unsettled.

'I don't understand . . . If he has evidence . . .'

'He will . . .'

'But how?'

'What do I know? . . . He'll find something . . .'

'To shift the guilt from himself?'

But Maigret dropped the conversation, murmuring:
'Do you have a light? . . . That's twenty matches that . . .'
'I don't smoke!'
And Machère wasn't exactly sure that he heard him say:
'I should have suspected as much . . .'

5. Maigret's Evening

The rain had started falling at about midday. At dusk, it was hammering loudly on the cobbles. By eight o'clock it was a deluge.

The streets of Givet were deserted. The barges gleamed along the quay. Maigret, the collar of his overcoat turned up, hurried towards the Flemish house, pushed the door open, set off the bell that was becoming familiar to him, and breathed in the warm smell of the grocery.

It was at this time of day that Germaine Piedboeuf had come into the shop, on 3 January, and no one had seen her again since then.

The inspector noticed for the first time that the kitchen was separated from the shop only by a glass door. It was decorated with a tulle curtain, so that one could vaguely make out the outlines of the figures.

Someone got up.

'Don't let me disturb you!' Maigret exclaimed.

And he went into the kitchen, walking in on the normal daily routine. It was Madame Peeters who had got up to go to the shop. Her husband was in his wicker armchair, still so close to the stove that one might have worried that he was going to catch fire. In his hand he held a meerschaum pipe with a long cherry-wood stem. But he wasn't smoking any more. His eyes were closed. Regular breaths issued from his half-open lips.

As to Anna, she was sitting at the sanded white wooden table, which had been polished by the years. She was doing some calculations in a little notebook.

'Bring the inspector to the dining room, Anna . . .'

'No!' he protested. 'I'm just passing through . . .'

'Give me your coat . . .'

And Maigret noticed the Madame Peeters had a beautiful, serious voice, deep and warm, a faint Flemish accent making it all the more delightful.

'You will have a cup of coffee!'

He wanted to know what she had been doing before he got there. At her place he saw steel-rimmed glasses and the day's newspaper.

The old man's breath seemed to provide a rhythm to the life of the house. Anna closed her notebook, put a cap on the pencil, got up and went to fetch a cup from a shelf.

'You will forgive me . . .' she murmured.

'I hoped to meet your sister, Maria.'

Madame Peeters nodded sadly. Anna explained:

'You won't see her for a few days, unless you pay her a visit in Namur. One of her colleagues, who also lives in Givet, came just now . . . Marie was getting off the train, this morning, when she sprained her ankle . . .'

'Where is she?'

'At the school . . . They have a room for her there . . .'

Madame Peeters sighed, still nodding:

'I don't know what we've done to offend the Lord!'

'And Joseph?'

'He won't be back before Saturday. Although that's only tomorrow . . .'

'Your cousin Marguerite hasn't paid you a visit?'

'No! I saw her at vespers . . .'

Boiling coffee was poured into the cup. Madame Peeters went out and came back in with a little glass, a bottle of genever.

'It's old Schiedam.'

He sat down. He didn't expect to find anything out. Perhaps even his presence was barely relevant to the case.

The house reminded him of an investigation he had conducted in Holland, but with differences that he was unable to define. There was the same calm, the same heaviness in the air, the same sensation that the atmosphere was not fluid, but formed a solid body that one would break by moving.

From time to time the wicker of the armchair creaked even though the old man hadn't moved. And his breathing still provided a rhythm for life, for the conversation.

Anna said something in Flemish, and Maigret, who had learned some words in Delfzijl, more or less understood:

'You should have given him a bigger glass . . .'

Every so often a man in clogs passed along the quay. The rain could be heard hammering on the front window.

'You told me it was raining, didn't you? As hard as it is today? . . .'

'Yes . . . I think so . . .'

And the two women, sitting down again, watched him pick up his glass and bring it to his lips.

Anna didn't have her mother's fine features, nor her

benevolent, indulgent smile. As usual, she didn't take her eyes off Maigret.

Had she noticed that the portrait was missing from her room? Probably not! If she had, she would have been upset.

'We've been here for thirty years, inspector . . .' said Madame Peeters. 'My husband set up as a basket-maker, in this very house; we added a second storey later on . . .'

Maigret was thinking about something else, about Anna, five years younger, going with Gérard Piedboeuf to the Rochefort caves.

What had driven her into her companion's arms? Why had she given herself? What had she thought afterwards? . . .

He had a sense that it was the only affair in her life, that she would never have any others . . .

The rhythm of life in this house was like a magic spell. The genever put a dull heat in Maigret's skull. He noticed the slightest little noises, the creaks of the armchair, the old man's snores, the drops of rain on a window-sill . . .

'You should play me that piece you played to me this morning again . . .' he said to Anna.

And as she hesitated, her mother pressed her:

'Yes indeed! . . . She plays well, doesn't she? . . . She had lessons for six years, three times a week, with the best teacher in Givet . . .'

The girl left the kitchen. The two doors remained open between her and the rest of the family. The piano lid banged open.

A few lazy notes with the right hand.

'She should sing . . .' murmured Madame Peeters. 'Marguerite sings better . . . There was even talk of her taking lessons at the Conservatoire . . .'

The notes filled the empty, echoing house. The old man didn't wake up, and his wife, worried that he might drop his pipe, delicately took it from his hands and hung it on a nail in the wall.

What was Maigret still doing there? He had nothing to find out. Madame Peeters listened, looking at her newspaper without daring to pick it up. Anna gradually accompanied herself with her left hand. Maigret guessed that it was at this table that Maria usually corrected her pupils' homework.

And that was all!

Except that the whole town was accusing the Peeters of killing Germaine Piedboeuf, on an evening just like this one!

Maigret gave a start at the sound of the shop bell. For a moment he felt as though he were three weeks younger, that Joseph's mistress was going to come in and claim the money for her keep, the hundred francs that she was paid each month to look after the child.

It was a sailor in an oilskin, who held out a small bottle to Madame Peeters, and she filled it with genever.

'Eight francs!'

'Belgian?'

'French! Ten Belgian francs . . .'

Maigret got up and walked across the shop.

'Are you leaving already?'

'I'll come back tomorrow.'

Outside, he saw the sailor returning to his boat. He turned towards the house. With its big, illuminated window it looked like a stage set, particularly because of the music it exhaled, sweet and sentimental.

Wasn't Anna's voice mingled with it?

. . . But you will return to me,
O my handsome betrothed . . .

Maigret waded about in the mud, and the rain fell so heavily that his pipe went out.

Now the whole of Givet seemed like a stage set. Now that the sailor was back on his boat, there wasn't a soul outside.

Nothing but the filtered lights at a few windows. And the noise of the Meuse in spate that gradually drowned out the song of the piano.

When he had walked 200 metres, he was able to see, at the end of the stage, both the Flemish house and, in the foreground, the other house, the one where the Piedboeufs lived.

There was no light upstairs. But the corridor was lit. The midwife must have been alone with the child.

Maigret was in a bad mood. He didn't often feel the pointlessness of his efforts to such an extent.

What had he come to do here, in the end? He wasn't on duty! People were accusing the Flemings of killing a young woman. But they couldn't even be sure that she was dead!

Might she not, weary of her wretched life in Givet, be in Brussels, Reims, Nancy or Paris, drinking in some brasserie or other with some friends she had met?

And even if she was dead, had she been killed? Discouraged, might she not have been drawn by the muddy river as she left the grocery?

No proof! No clue! Machère would go as far as he could, but he wouldn't find anything, so that one day the public prosecutor's office would decide to close the case.

So why was Maigret getting drenched on this foreign stage?

Just in front of him, on the other side of the Meuse, he saw the factory, whose courtyard was lit only by an electric light. Very near the gate, a guardroom with a light.

Old Piedboeuf had gone to work. What did he do there all night?

And then, without knowing quite why, Maigret, hands deep in his pockets, made his way towards the bridge. In the café where he had had a hot rum in the morning a dozen sailors and tugboat-owners were talking so loudly that they could be heard from the quay. But he didn't stop.

The wind vibrated the steel girders of the bridge which replaced the stone bridge that had been destroyed during the war.

And, on the opposite shore, the quay hadn't even been paved. You had to wade through mud. A roaming dog pressed itself against the whitewashed wall.

A small door was built into the closed gate. And

immediately Maigret saw Piedboeuf pressing his face to the glass of the guardroom.

'Good evening!'

The man was wearing an old army jacket that he had had dyed black. He too was smoking a pipe. And, in the middle of the room, he had a little stove whose chimney, after two bends, went into the wall.

'You know you're not allowed . . .'

'To come here at night! That's fine!'

A wooden bench. A chair with a rush seat. Maigret's overcoat was already starting to steam.

'Do you stay in this room all night?'

'Excuse me! I have to do three rounds of the courtyards and the workshops.'

From a distance, his big grey moustache might have misled. Close up, he was a timid man, ready to collapse at any moment, with the keenest sense of his humble condition.

Maigret intimidated him. He didn't know what to say to him.

'So, you always live on your own . . . Here at night . . . In your bed in the morning . . . And in the afternoon . . . ?'

'I do the garden!'

'The midwife's garden?'

'Yes . . . we share the vegetables . . .'

Maigret noticed some rounded shapes in the ashes. He prodded them with the tip of the poker and discovered some potatoes in their skins. He understood. He imagined the man, all on his own, in the middle of the night, eating potatoes and gazing into the void.

'Does your son never come and see you at the factory?'

'Never!'

Here too the drops of rain were falling one by one outside the door, giving an irregular rhythm to life.

'Do you really think your daughter was murdered?'

The man didn't reply straight away. He didn't know where to look.

'Since the moment that Gérard . . .'

And suddenly, with a sob in the depths of his throat:

'She wouldn't have killed herself . . . She wouldn't have left . . .'

It was unexpectedly tragic. The man mechanically filled his pipe.

'If I didn't think that those people . . .'

'Do you know Joseph Peeters well?'

And Piedboeuf looked away.

'I knew he wouldn't marry her . . . They are rich people . . . And we . . .'

There was a fine electric clock on the wall, the only luxury in this cabin. Opposite, a blackboard on which someone had written in chalk: *Not hiring*.

Lastly, near the door, a complicated apparatus with a big wheel for recording the time at which the workforce arrived and left.

'Time for my round . . .'

Maigret almost suggested going with him, to reach further into this man's life. Piedboef put on a shapeless oilskin that flapped against his heels and picked up from a corner a hurricane lamp that was already lit, so that all he had to do was lengthen its wick.

'I don't understand why you're against us . . . Perhaps it's natural, after all! . . . Gérard says that . . .'

But the rain interrupted them, because they had reached the courtyard. Piedboeuf guided his guest to the gate that he was going to close before he did his round.

One more source of astonishment for the inspector. From there he could see a landscape cut into equal slices by the iron bars: the barges moored on the other side of the river, the Flemish house and the illuminated front window, the quay where electric lights drew circles of light every fifty metres.

From here you had a very clear view of the customs building and the Café des Mariniers . . .

Most importantly, you could see the corner of the alleyway with the Piedboeufs' house second on the left.

The third of January . . .

'Has your wife been dead for a long time?'

'Twelve years next month . . . She suffered with her chest . . .'

'What does Gérard do at this time of day?'

The lamp dangled at the end of the night watchman's arm. He had already put a big key in the lock. A train whistled in the distance.

'He must be in town . . .'

'You don't know which side?'

'The young people tend to meet at the Café de la Mairie!'

And Maigret hurried off again through the rain, into the darkness. It wasn't an investigation. It had no starting point, no foundation.

There were only a handful of humans each getting on with their own lives in the little windswept town.

Perhaps they were all sincere. But perhaps one of them concealed a tormented soul, frightened to death at the thought of the bulky form roaming these streets at night.

Maigret passed in front of his hotel without going in. Through the windows he could see Inspector Machère, holding forth in the middle of a group that included the landlord. It looked like the fourth or fifth round of drinks. The landlord had just bought his.

Machère, very animated, was waving his arms around and must have been saying:

'These detective chief inspectors who come from Paris have notions of themselves . . .'

And they were talking about the Flemings! They were tearing them to shreds!

At the end of a narrow street there was quite a spacious square. On one corner, a café with a white frontage and three well-lit windows: Café de la Mairie.

A noise that welcomed you as soon as you opened the door. A zinc counter. Tables. Card-players at red baize tables. Smoke from pipes and cigarettes and a sharp smell of stale beer.

'Two beers, two!'

The sound of counters on the marble tabletop near the cash register. The waiter's white apron.

'Over here!'

Maigret sat down at the first table he came to, and first saw Gérard Piedboeuf in one of the tarnished mirrors in the bar. He was very animated, like Machère. He stopped short as he saw Maigret, and his foot must have touched those of his companions.

One male companion, two female. There were four of them at the same table. The young people were the same age. The women were probably lowly factory girls.

They all fell silent. Even the card-players at the other tables called out their points in an undertone, and their eyes were fixed on the new arrival.

'A beer!'

Maigret lit his pipe, and put his dripping bowler hat down on the brown moleskin banquette.

'One beer, just one!'

And Gérard Piedboeuf assumed an ironic and contemptuous smile and muttered under his breath:

'The friend of the Flemings . . .'

He had been drinking too. His pupils were too shiny. His purple lips offset the pallor of his complexion. It was clear that he was very excited. He was playing to the gallery. He was trying to find something to say to shock his lady companions.

'You realize, Ninie, when you're rich you won't have to worry about the police any more . . .'

His friend gave him a nudge to make him shut up, but it only made him more worked up.

'What? Aren't we allowed to say what we want any more? . . . I repeat that the police are at the disposal of the rich, but as soon as you're poor . . .'

He was pale. Basically he had frightened himself with

his words, but he wanted to preserve the halo that his attitude gave him.

Maigret removed the foam that covered his glass and took a great gulp of beer. The card-players could be heard murmuring, to break the silence:

'A flush . . .'

'Four jacks . . .'

'Your deal!'

'I'll cut!'

And the two little factory workers who didn't dare to turn and look at the inspector arranged themselves so that they could see him in the mirror.

'You would think it was a crime to be French in France! Particularly if you're poor as well . . .'

At the till, the landlord frowned and turned towards Maigret, who didn't look at him, hoping to indicate to him that the young man was drunk.

'Spades! . . . And spades again! . . . Eh? You weren't expecting that . . .'

'People who have made their fortune by smuggling!' Gérard went on, keen to be heard by the whole bar. 'Everyone in Givet knows! Before the war it was cigars and lace . . . Now, since alcohol is forbidden in Belgium, they serve genever to the Flemish sailors . . . Which allows their son to become a lawyer . . . Ha ha! He'll need it, to defend himself! . . .'

And Maigret stayed alone at his table, the focus of all the customers' attention. He hadn't taken off his overcoat. His shoulders were glistening with rain.

The landlord became agitated, foreseeing trouble, and approached the inspector:

'Please ignore him . . . He's been drinking . . . And the grief . . .'

'Let's go, Gérard!' the little woman beside the young man murmured anxiously.

'So that he thinks I'm scared of him?'

He still had his back to Maigret. Each could see the other only in the mirrors.

Now the other customers were only playing for the sake of appearances, and forgetting to mark the points on their tiles.

'A brandy, please! . . . Time for a drink! . . .'

The landlord almost refused but didn't dare, given that Maigret was still pretending not to notice him.

'It's a complete outrage! . . . That's what it is! . . . These people take our daughters and kill them as soon as they've had enough of them . . . And the police . . .'

Maigret imagined old Piedboeuf, in his dyed uniform, doing the rounds of the workshops by the light of his hurricane lamp, coming back to his nice warm corner to eat his potatoes.

Opposite, the Piedboeuf house: the midwife must have put the child to bed and was waiting for her own bedtime, reading or doing some knitting.

Then, further off, the Flemish grocery, old Peeters being woken and led to his bedroom. Madame Peeters lowering the shutters, Anna, all by herself, undressing in her room . . .

And the barges slumbering in the current that stretched the moorings, made the rudders creak and the dinghies collide . . .

'Another beer!'

Maigret's voice was calm. He smoked slowly, blowing puffs of smoke towards the ceiling.

'You'll all have noticed that he's taunting me! . . . Because he is taunting me . . .'

The landlord was desperate and had run out of ideas. A scandal was erupting.

For, at those last words, Gérard had got to his feet and was standing in front of Maigret at last. His features were drawn, his lips contorted in anger.

'I tell you that he's only come here to annoy us! . . . Look at him! . . . He's laughing at us, because I've had a drink . . . Or rather because we haven't got any money . . .'

Maigret didn't move. It was insane! He was as motionless as the marble of his table. He had his hand on his glass. He was still smoking.

'Diamonds trumps!' said someone optimistically, in the hope of creating a diversion.

And then Gérard took the cards from the card-players' table and threw them across the room.

Suddenly half the customers were on their feet, not daring to come forwards, but ready to intervene.

Maigret sat where he was. Maigret smoked.

'But look at him! He's taunting us! He knows my sister was murdered . . .'

The landlord didn't know where to put himself. The two little women at Gérard's table looked at each other anxiously, and had already measured the distance they were from the door.

'He doesn't dare say anything! You'll notice that he

doesn't dare open his mouth! He's scared! Yes, he's scared that the truth will come out!'

'I swear to you that he's been drinking!' the landlord cried, seeing Maigret get to his feet.

Too late! Of all of them, it was probably Gérard who was the most frightened.

That dark, wet mass coming towards him . . .

He moved his hand briefly towards his pocket, and that movement was accompanied by a loud scream from a woman.

The young man was drawing a revolver. But Maigret caught it in mid-air with his hand. At the same time, he stuck his foot out and sent Gérard sprawling.

At most, one customer out of three knew what was happening. And yet now they had all got to their feet. The revolver was in Maigret's hand. Gérard got back to his feet, with a fierce expression on his face, humiliated by his defeat.

And while the inspector put the gun in his pocket, with a gesture as calm as it was natural, the young man panted:

'So are you going to arrest me, then?'

He wasn't standing up yet. He was pulling himself up with his hands. It was pitiful.

'Go to bed!' Maigret said slowly.

As Gérard seemed not to understand, he added:

'Open the door!'

There was a gust of fresh air in the stifling atmosphere. Maigret held Gérard's shoulder and pushed him towards the pavement.

'Go to bed!'

And the door closed again. There was one person fewer in the bar: Gérard Piedboeuf.

'He's blind drunk!' muttered Maigret, sitting back in front of the beer he had just begun.

The customers didn't know what they were supposed to do. Some of them had sat down in their seats again. Others were hesitating.

Then Maigret, after taking a sip of beer, sighed:

'It doesn't matter!'

Then, turning to his neighbour, who didn't know what was going on, he added:

'You were saying that diamonds were trumps . . .'

6. The Hammer

Maigret had decided to sleep in, less out of laziness than for want of anything better to do. It was about ten o'clock when he had an unpleasant awakening.

First of all there was a violent knocking at his door, which he hated more than anything. Then, his senses still befuddled, he made out the rattle of rain on the balcony.

'Who is it?'

'Machère.'

He called out his name as if he were making a triumphant bugle call.

'Come in! Go and open the curtains . . .'

And Maigret, still in bed, saw the dull light of a filthy day flowing in. Downstairs, a fisherwoman was negotiating with the hotel landlord.

'Some news! It came in this morning with the first post . . .'

'Just a moment! Would you please call downstairs for them to bring me up my breakfast, because there's no service bell . . .'

And without leaving his bed, Maigret lit a pipe that lay ready filled within his reach.

'News about whom?'

'About Germaine Piedboeuf.'

'Dead?'

'Dead as can be!'

Machère announced this with delight, taking a letter from his pocket, four large-format pages decorated with administrative stamps.

> Issued by the Public Prosecutor's Office of Huy to the Ministry of the Interior in Brussels.
> Issued by the Ministry of the Interior to the Sûreté in Paris.
> Issued by the Sûreté to the Flying Squad in Nancy.
> Issued to Inspector Machère, in Givet . . .

'Keep it short, will you?'

'Well, in a few words, she was pulled from the Meuse in Huy, about a hundred kilometres from here. Five days ago . . . They didn't immediately connect it with the request for information that I'd made to the Belgian police . . . But I'll read it to you . . .'

'Can I come in?'

It was the chambermaid with coffee and croissants. When she had left, Machère continued:

'"This twenty-sixth of January, in the year nineteen . . ."'

'No, old man! Get straight to the point . . .'

'Well! It seems almost certain that she was murdered. It's not just conjecture, it's a material fact . . . Listen: "The body, as far as one can judge, must have been in the water for between three weeks and a month . . . Her state of . . ."'

'Keep it short!' grunted Maigret, who was eating.

'". . . decomposition . . ."'

'I know! The conclusions! And most of all, no description!'

'There's a whole page . . .'

'Of what?'

'Of description . . . Well, if you say so . . . It doesn't come to a definitive conclusion . . . And yet one thing is certain: it's that Germaine Piedboeuf was dead long before she was put in the water . . . The doctor says: "two or three days before . . ."'

Maigret was still dipping his croissant in his coffee, eating and looking at the rectangle of the window, and Machère thought he wasn't listening to him.

'Aren't you interested in this?'

'Go on.'

'There's the detailed account of the post-mortem . . . Do you want me to . . . ? No? . . . Well! Let me tell you the most interesting part . . . The skull of the corpse had been completely shattered, the doctors are fairly sure that death was due to this fracture, produced with a blunt instrument, like a hammer or a lump of iron . . .'

Maigret put one leg out of bed, then the other, and looked at himself in the mirror before beginning to soap his cheeks with his shaving brush. As he was shaving, Inspector Machère reread the typed report that he was holding.

'Don't you think that's extraordinary? Not the hammer blow? I'm talking about the fact that the body wasn't thrown into the water until two or three days after death . . . I will have to pay the Flemings another visit . . .'

'Do you have the list of clothes that Germaine Piedboeuf was wearing?'

'Yes . . . Wait . . . Black buckled shoes, quite badly worn . . . Black stockings . . . Poor-quality pink underwear . . . Black serge dress, no brand . . .'

'Is that all? No coat?'

'Hang on! You're quite right . . .'

'It was the third of January . . . It was raining . . . It was cold . . .'

Machère's face darkened. He grunted without explaining himself:

'Obviously!'

'Obviously what?'

'She didn't get on well enough with the Peeters that they would invite her to make herself at home . . . On the other hand, I don't see why the murderer would have taken off her coat . . . Or else he would have undressed her completely to make identification more difficult . . .'

Maigret washed himself very noisily, even splashing Machère, although he was in the middle of the room.

'Have the Piedboeufs been told?'

'Not yet . . . I thought you might take charge of that . . .'

'Not at all! I'm not on duty! Pretend you're on your own, old man!'

And he looked for the button of his collar, finished dressing and pushed Machère towards the door.

'I need to go out . . . See you later . . .'

He didn't know where he was going. He went out for the sake of it, or rather to immerse himself in the atmosphere of the town. By chance he stopped in front of a brass plaque that announced:

Doctor Van de Weert
Consultations from ten o'clock until midday

A few minutes later he was led past the three patients sitting in the waiting room and found himself in the presence of a small man with the pink skin of a child and hair the same white as Madame Peeters.

'Nothing unpleasant, I hope?'

He rubbed his hands as he spoke. He exuded hearty optimism from every pore.

'My daughter told me you'd agreed to . . .'

'First of all I would like to ask you a question. How much strength would it take to smash a woman's skull with a hammer blow?'

The bafflement of the little man, whose belly was crossed by a fat watch chain, and who wore a jacket that had seen better days, was a delight.

'A skull? . . . How should I know? . . . I've never had the occasion, in Givet . . .'

'Do you think, for example, that a woman might be capable . . .'

He panicked, he gesticulated.

'A woman? . . . But this is madness! . . . A woman would never think of . . .'

'Are you a widower, Monsieur Van de Weert?'

'For twenty years! Luckily my daughter . . .'

'What do you think of Joseph Peeters?'

'But . . . he's an excellent fellow! . . . I would rather he had chosen medicine, because he would have taken over my practice . . . But, of course, since he's good at law . . . It is a remarkable subject . . .'

'From the health point of view?'

'Very good! Very good! A bit tired from working doggedly, and by his growth . . .'

'The Peeters have no defect?'

'A defect?'

So great was his stupefaction, he might never have heard of such a thing.

'You are incredible, inspector! I don't understand! You've seen my cousin. She's built to live for a century . . .'

'Your daughter too?'

'She's more delicate . . . She takes after her mother . . . But allow me to offer you a cigar . . .'

A true Fleming like the ones one sees in the posters advertising a brand of genever, a Fleming with full lips and clear eyes, proclaiming the simplicity of his soul.

'In the end, Mademoiselle Marguerite had to marry her cousin.'

His face darkened slightly.

'Sooner or later, of course! . . . Had it not been for that unfortunate affair . . .'

As far as he was concerned, it was only unfortunate!

'They just didn't grasp that the best thing to do was to accept a small sum for the child and, if possible, to move to a different town . . . I think it's the brother in particular who has a poor character . . .'

No! You couldn't hold it against him! He was sincere! Naive by virtue of his sincerity!

'Not to mention the fact that there's no evidence that the child is Joseph's . . . He would have been far better off in a sanatorium, with his mother . . .'

'So your daughter was waiting . . .'

And Van de Weert smiled.

'She has loved him since she was fourteen or fifteen . . . Isn't that lovely? . . . Was I supposed to stand in their way? . . . Do you have a light? . . . If you ask my opinion, there isn't even anything to get worked up about . . . The young woman, who was always a little manhunter, has followed a new boyfriend somewhere or other . . . And her brother took advantage of the fact to try and make himself some money . . .'

He didn't ask Maigret's advice. He was sure that his opinion was right. He listened out for vague sounds from the waiting room, where his clients were bound to be getting impatient.

Then Maigret, calmly, and with the same innocent expression as the doctor, asked one last question:

'Do you think that Mademoiselle Marguerite is her cousin's mistress?'

Perhaps Van de Weert was on the point of losing his temper. His forehead turned red. But what prevailed was sadness in the face of such incomprehension.

'Marguerite? . . . You're mad! . . . Who could have come up with such a thing? . . . Marguerite, the . . . the . . .'

And Maigret, who was already holding the door handle, left without even smiling. The house smelled of both chemicals and cooking. The servant who opened the door to the clients was as fresh as if she had just emerged from a hot bath.

But outside it was all rain and mud again, and passing lorries splashed the pavements.

It was Saturday. Joseph Peeters was due to arrive in the afternoon and spend Sunday in Givet. At the Café des Mariniers they were engaged in a passionate discussion because the Department of Roads and Bridges had just announced that shipping traffic had resumed between the border and Maastricht.

Except that, given the strength of the current, the tugs were asking for fifteen francs a kilometre per ton, rather than ten. They had also learned that an arch of the Namur bridge had been obstructed by a barge loaded with stones that had broken its mooring and crashed into the pier.

'Any casualties?' asked Maigret.

'The wife and her son. The bargeman himself was in the bar, and by the time he got to the waterside his boat had already taken off!'

Gérard Piedboeuf passed by on his bicycle, coming back from the factory offices. And a few moments later Machère came back from the Flemish house, where he had gone to announce the news, rang the doorbell of the Piedboeuf house and found himself face to face with the midwife, who curtly let him in.

'So tell me about your indecent assault case.'

On most barges, the accommodation is cleaner than most people's houses. But that was not the case on the *Étoile Polaire*.

The bargeman had no wife. He was helped by a lad of about twenty who wasn't quite right in the head and who had epileptic seizures from time to time.

The cabin smelled like a barracks. The man was busy eating bread and sausage and drinking a litre of red wine.

He was less drunk than usual. He looked suspiciously at Maigret, and it was quite a long time before he decided to speak.

'It wasn't even an assault . . . I'd already slept with the girl two or three times . . . One evening, in the street, I meet her and, because I've been drinking, she turns me down . . . So I hit her . . . She screamed . . . Some cops happened to be passing by, and I knocked one of them down . . .'

'Five years?'

'Nearly. She denied that we'd had relations before . . . Some friends of mine came to court and said we had, but they only half believed them . . . Without the cop, who spent a fortnight in hospital, I'd have got off with a year, maybe even suspended . . .'

And he cut his bread with a penknife.

'Are you thirsty? . . . We might leave tomorrow . . . We're waiting to see if the bridge at Namur is cleared . . .'

'Now tell me why you made up the story of the woman you saw on the quay.'

'Me?'

He took some time to think and pretended to eat hungrily.

'Admit it, you didn't see anything at all!'

Maigret caught a flicker of joy in the other man's eyes.

'That's what you think? Well! I'm sure you're right!'

'Who asked you to give that statement?'

'Me?'

And he was still laughing. He spat his sausage skin out right in front of him.

'Where did you meet Gérard Piedboeuf?'

'Oh! I see . . .'

But he was face to face with a man as placid as himself.

'Did he give you something?'

'He bought some rounds . . .'

Then, suddenly, with a silent chuckle:

'Except it isn't true! I'm just saying that to please you . . . If you want me to tell the court the opposite, you just have to give me a sign . . .'

'What did you see exactly?'

'If I told you, you wouldn't believe me.'

'Tell me anyway!'

'Well! I saw a woman waiting . . . then a man came, and she threw herself into his arms . . .'

'Who was it?'

'How do you expect me to recognize them in the dark?'

'Where were you?'

'I was coming back from the bar . . .'

'And where did the couple go? To the Flemish house?'

'No! They went in the back way.'

'The back of what?'

'The back of the house . . . But if you don't think I'm telling the truth . . . I'm used to it, you understand! . . . They told so many stories at my trial . . . Even my lawyer, who was the worst liar of all . . .'

'Do you go and have a glass at the Flemish house from time to time?'

'Me? . . . They refuse to serve me, on the grounds that I once broke the scales by punching my fist down on them . . . They need customers who get off their faces without moving or saying anything . . .'

'Did Gérard Piedboeuf speak to you?'

'What did I tell you a moment ago?'

'That he'd asked you to say . . .'

'Well! That's the truth . . . And the truth, honest to God, is that I'll never tell you what I know, because I hate the cops, you as much as the others! . . . You can go and tell the judge . . . I'll swear you beat me, and I'll show them the marks . . . Which won't stop me offering you a glass of red wine, if your stomach can take it . . .'

At that very moment, Maigret looked him in the eyes and suddenly got to his feet.

'Show me around your boat!' he said curtly.

Surprise? Fear? Simple annoyance? Whatever it was, the man, his mouth full, pulled a face.

'What do you want to see?'

'One moment . . .'

And Maigret went outside and came back a few seconds later with a customs officer in an oilskin glistening with rain. The bargeman sniggered:

'I've already passed the inspection . . .'

Maigret was talking to the customs officer.

'You're used to it . . . I imagine all boats do a certain amount of smuggling . . .'

'Not a certain amount!'

'Where do they usually hide the goods?'

'It depends . . . In the old days they used to lock it up in waterproof boxes that they fastened under the boat . . . But now we put a chain under the hull, so they can't do that now . . . Under the floor too, sometimes, between the floor and the bottom . . . But we tend to make a few holes with a huge drill that you might have seen on the quay . . .'

'So?'

'Wait! What's your cargo?'

'Ironwork . . .'

'It would take too long . . .' grunted the customs officer. 'We'll have to look elsewhere . . .'

And Maigret didn't take his eyes off the bargeman. He hoped for a revealing glance towards some hiding place. The man was still eating, not hungrily, just to do something. He wasn't frightened. On the contrary, he sat firmly where he was.

'Get up!'

This time he obeyed with bad grace.

'Am I not allowed to sit down in my own place these days?'

On the chair there was a filthy cushion, which Maigret picked up. Three sides of the cushion were sewn normally. The fourth bore coarse stitches that hadn't been made by a seamstress.

'Thank you! I don't need you any more!' Maigret said to the customs man.

'You think he's smuggling?'

'Not in the slightest . . . Thank you . . .'

And he waited until the official reluctantly left.

'What is it?'

'Nothing at all!'

'Do you usually put things as hard as that in cushions?'

The stitches parted, revealing something black. And soon Maigret unfolded a little worn serge coat, full of creases.

It was the same serge described in the report from the Belgian public prosecutor's office. There was no label. The piece of clothing had been made by Germaine Piedboeuf herself.

But that wasn't the most interesting object. In the middle of the parcel there was a hammer, its handle polished with use.

'The funniest thing,' the bargeman muttered, 'is that you're making a big mistake . . . I haven't done anything! . . . I got those two things there out of the Meuse, on the fourth of January, first thing . . .'

'And you thought it was a good idea to put them in a safe place!'

'I'm starting to get used to it!' the man replied complacently. 'Are you arresting me?'

'Is that all you have to say?'

'That you're making a big mistake!'

'Are you still leaving tomorrow?'

'If you don't arrest me, it's very likely.'

It must have been the biggest surprise in the world to

see Maigret carefully making up the parcel again, slipping it under his overcoat and leaving without a word.

He watched him walk off in the rain, along the quay, passing in front of the customs man, who saluted him. Then he went back down into his cabin, shaking his head, and poured himself a drink.

7. *A Three-Hour Gap*

When Maigret arrived at his hotel for lunch, the landlord told him the postman had turned up with a recorded delivery letter at his address but hadn't wanted to leave it.

It was like a signal for a thousand petty concerns to get together and start harassing a man. As soon as he sat down, the inspector asked after his colleague. No one had seen him. He had them call his hotel. He was told that he had left half an hour before.

It didn't matter. Maigret didn't even have the power to give instructions to Machère. But he would have liked to suggest that he keep an eye on the bargeman.

At two o'clock he was at the post office, where he was handed the recorded delivery letter. It was a silly story. Some furniture he had bought and refused to pay for because it wasn't what he'd ordered. The supplier had sent him a formal demand.

He had to spend half an hour writing his reply, then a letter to his wife to give her instructions on the subject.

No sooner had he finished than he was called to the phone. It was the head of the Police Judiciaire asking him when he would be back and requesting that he send some details about two or three cases currently under way.

Outside, it was still raining. The café floor was covered with sawdust. There was no one there at that time of day, and the waiter was taking advantage of the fact to get on with his own correspondence.

One ridiculous little detail: Maigret hated writing on marble tables, and there were no others.

'Please call the Hôtel de la Gare and find out if anyone's seen the inspector.'

Maigret was in a vaguely bad mood, all the more aggravating because it had no serious cause. Two or three times he went and pressed his forehead against the misted window. The sky was becoming a little clearer, the drops of rain less frequent. But the muddy quay was still deserted.

At about four o'clock he heard a blast from a whistle. He ran to the door and saw a tug, belching out thick steam for the first time since the spate had begun.

The current was still violent. When the tug, slender and light, a thoroughbred in comparison with the barges, came away from the shore, it literally reared up, and for a moment looked as if it was going to be dragged away by the flood.

A new whistle-blast, more strident this time. And it turned into the current. A cable stretched behind it. A first barge broke away from the block of waiting boats and drifted across the Meuse as two men pulled with all their might on the helm.

In the doorways of the cafés, customers had gathered to witness the manoeuvre, which took no more than six minutes. Two or three barges entered the struggle in turn, formed a semi-circle and suddenly, at the sound of a whistle, vibrant with pride, the tug set off towards Belgium, while the barges behind it did their best to stay in a straight line.

The *Étoile Polaire* was not part of the train.

> . . . and consequently I ask you to be so kind as to collect from my home at Boulevard Richard Lenoir the furniture which . . .

Maigret wrote unusually slowly, as if his fingers were too big for the pen that they were crushing on to the paper. By contrast, this produced handwriting that was small but fat which, from a distance, looked like a series of stains.

'Monsieur Peeters going past on his motorbike . . .' announced the waiter, who was lighting the lamps and drawing the curtains over the big window.

It was half past four.

'It takes courage to cover 200 kilometres in weather like that! He's muddy from head to toe!'

'Albert! The telephone!' cried the landlady.

Maigret signed the letter and put it in an envelope.

'It's for you, inspector! From Paris . . .'

'Hello! . . . Hello! . . . Yes, it's me . . .'

And Maigret tried to rein in his bad mood. It was his wife on the phone, asking him when he was coming back.

'Hello . . . They came for the furniture . . .'

'I know! I'll do what needs to be done . . .'

'There's also a letter from the English colleague who . . .'

'Yes, darling! It doesn't matter . . .'

'Is it cold there? Cover up well . . . You haven't quite recovered from your cold and . . .'

Why did he feel almost painful impatience? A vague impression. He felt as if he was missing something, wasting his time in this cabin.

'I'll be in Paris in three or four days.'

'Is that all!'

'Yes . . . Lots of love . . . Goodbye . . .'

In the café, he asked where he would find a post box.

'Just on the corner of the street, by the tobacconist's.'

It was dark outside. All that could be seen of the Meuse was the reflections of the street lights. Against the trunk of a tree, Maigret noticed a figure that made him start. It wasn't the sort of weather to go for a walk in the rain and the wind.

He put the letter in the box, turned round and saw the figure detaching itself from the tree. He walked off, and the stranger started walking behind him.

It was quick work! A few hasty steps back and Maigret grabbed the man by the collar.

'What are you doing here?'

He was holding him a bit too tightly. The stranger's face was flushed. Maigret relaxed his grip.

'Speak!'

Something shocked him, he didn't know what. That evasive gaze was awkward, even more awkward than the smile on the man's face.

'Aren't you the steward on the *Étoile Polaire*?'

The man nodded his head delightedly.

'Were you tailing me?'

There was a mixture of fear and gaiety on the man's long face. Had the sailor not confessed to Maigret that his steward was simple-minded and prey to epileptic seizures?

'Don't laugh! Tell me what you're doing here . . .'

'I'm watching you.'

'Was it your boss who told you to keep me under surveillance?

It was impossible to be brutal with this poor wretch, all the more pitiful because of his age. He was twenty. He didn't shave, but his sparse beard, of very fine hairs, wasn't even as long as a centimetre. His mouth was twice as big as a normal mouth.

'Don't beat me . . .'

'Come!'

Some barges had changed places. For the first time in weeks there was activity on board, because they were preparing to leave. Women could be seen going for provisions. Customs men were walking around, boarding the boats.

The *Étoile Polaire*, once the other boats had left, was isolated, and her bows were some distance from the shore. There was a light in the cabin.

'You go ahead!'

He had to walk along a gangway that consisted only of a sagging and unstable plank.

There was no one on board, even though the paraffin lamp was lit.

'Where does your boss keep his Sunday best?'

For Maigret saw an unusual degree of chaos.

The steward opened a cupboard and was amazed by what he saw. The clothes that the bargeman had been wearing in the morning could be seen lying on the floor.

'And his money?'

Gestures of furious denial. The idiot didn't know! The money was hidden!

'It's all right! You can stay here.'

Maigret went outside, his head down, and bumped into a customs man.

'You haven't seen the man from the *Étoile Polaire*?'

'No! Isn't he on board? I thought he was supposed to be leaving first thing.'

'Does he own the boat?'

'Far from it! It belongs to one of his cousins, who lives in Flémalle. An eccentric like himself . . .'

'What does he earn from the barge?'

'Six hundred francs a month? Perhaps a bit more with the smuggling . . . But not much . . .'

The Flemish house was lit up. There were lights on not only in the windows of the shop, but also on the first floor.

A few minutes later, the bell of the grocery rang. Maigret wiped the soles of his shoes on the mat, and called out to Madame Peeters, who was already running from the kitchen:

'Don't let me bother you!'

The first person he saw, when he was ushered into the dining room, was Marguerite Van de Weert, who was flicking through a musical score.

She was more diaphanous than ever in her pale-blue satin dress, and she gave Maigret a welcoming smile.

'Have you come to see Joseph?'

'Isn't he here?'

'He's gone upstairs to change . . . It's insane to go out on a motorbike in weather like this! Especially him, when his health is already delicate and his exams are taking such a toll on him . . .'

It wasn't love! It was adoration! It was as if she was capable of spending hours not moving, looking at this young man!

What was it about him that inspired such feelings? Did his sister not speak of him in almost identical terms?

'Is Anna with him?'

'She's getting his clothes ready for him.'

'What about you? Have you been here for long?'

'An hour.'

'Did you know that Joseph Peeters was going to come?'

Slight unease. It only lasted a second and she continued straight away:

'He comes every Saturday at the same time.'

'Is there a phone in the house?'

'Not here! At home, of course! My father needs it all the time.'

He was starting to dislike her, he didn't know why. Or more precisely she was starting to get on his nerves! He didn't like her babyish ways, her deliberately childish way of talking, her expression, which was supposed to be candid.

'Wait a second! Here he comes . . .'

And sure enough, there was the sound of footsteps on the stairs. Joseph Peeters came into the dining room, quite clean, quite neat, his hair still bearing the traces of a wet comb.

'Been here long, inspector?'

He didn't dare to hold out his hand. He turned towards Marguerite.

'And you haven't offered him anything to drink?'

In the shop, several people were talking Flemish. Anna arrived in turn, peaceful, and bowed as she must have learned at the convent.

'Is it true, inspector, that there was a scene last night in a café in the town? I know that people always exaggerate . . . But . . . sit down! Joseph! Go and get something to drink . . .'

There was a coal-nut fire in the hearth. The piano was open.

Maigret tried to identify an impression that he had had since he arrived, but every time he thought he was on the point of reaching his destination, his thought became elusive.

Something had changed. But he didn't know what.

And he was in a bad mood. He had the blank face, the stubborn brow of his bad days. In fact, he wanted to do something incongruous just to disrupt all the harmony that surrounded him.

It was Anna more than anyone who inspired this confused feeling in him. She was still wearing the same grey dress that gave her figure the motionless appearance of a statue.

Had events really taken their toll on her? Her movements didn't cause a ripple in the folds of her clothes.

She was like a character in a Greek tragedy, lost in the mean everyday life of the little border town.

'Do you often help out with the . . . business?'

He hadn't dared to say: in the shop.

'Often! I stand in for my mother.'

'And do you serve drinks as well?'

She didn't smile. She just looked amazed.

'Why not?'

'Sometimes sailors are drunk, aren't they? They must get very familiar, perhaps bothersome?'

'Not here!'

And again she was a statue! She was sure of herself!

'Would you prefer some port or . . . ?'

'I'd rather have a glass of that Schiedam you offered me the other day.'

'Go and ask Mother for the bottle of "vieux système", Joseph.'

And Joseph obeyed.

Did Maigret need to change the hierarchical order he had imagined, which was this: first Joseph, the real god of the family. Then Anna. Then Maria. Then Madame Peeters, devoted to the grocery. And last of all the father, asleep in his armchair?

Anna, smoothly, seemed to be assuming first place.

'Have you found out anything new, inspector? Did you see that the boats were starting to leave? River traffic has been re-established to Liège, perhaps as far as Maastricht . . . In two days there will only be three or four barges at a time here . . .'

Why was she saying this?

'No, Marguerite! The stemmed glasses.'

For Marguerite was fetching glasses from the dresser.

Maigret was still tormented by his need to break the equilibrium, and he took advantage of the fact that Joseph was in the shop, his cousin busy choosing glasses, to show Anna the portrait of Gérard Piedboeuf.

'I need to talk to you about it!' he said under his breath.

He looked at her fervently. But if he hoped to disturb her calm expression, he was to be disappointed. She merely made a sign as if from one accomplice to another. A sign that said: 'Yes . . . Later . . .'

And to her brother as he came in:

'Are there still a lot of people?'

'Five people.'

Straight away, Anna displayed a grasp of nuance. The bottle that Joseph brought had a slender tin pipe in it, meaning that the liquid could be poured without wasting a drop.

Before serving him, the girl took out this accessory, indicating that it was unseemly in a drawing room, with guests.

Maigret warmed his glass in the hollow of his hand for a moment.

'To your good health!' he said.

'To your good health!' repeated Joseph Peeters, who was the only one drinking.

'We now have proof that Germaine Piedboeuf was murdered.'

Only Marguerite uttered a little startled cry, the sort of girlish cry that one hears in the theatre.

'That's terrible!'

'I heard, but I didn't want to believe it!' said Anna. 'It's going to make our situation even more difficult, isn't it?'

'Or easier! Particularly if I manage to prove that your brother wasn't in Givet on the third of January.'

'Why?'

'Because Germaine Piedboeuf was killed with blows from a hammer.'

'My God! Don't say any more!'

It was Marguerite who got up, very pale, on the brink of fainting.

'I have the hammer in my pocket.'

'No! Please . . . Don't show us . . .'

But Anna stayed calm. She addressed her brother.

'Has your friend come back?' she asked.

'Yesterday.'

Then she explained to the inspector:

'It's the friend he spent the evening of the third with in a café in Nancy . . . He had set off for Marseille, about ten days ago, after his mother died . . . He's just come back . . .'

'Your good health!' replied Maigret, emptying his glass.

And he picked up the bottle and poured himself another drink. Every now and again the bell rang. Or there was the sound of a little shovel pouring sugar into a paper bag and the bump of the scales.

'Isn't your sister any better?'

'They think she'll be able to get up on Monday or Tuesday. But she probably won't be back here for a long time.'

'Is she getting married?'

'No! She wants to become a nun. It's an idea that she's been toying with for a long time.'

How could Maigret tell that something was happening in the shop? The noises were the same, perhaps less loud. But a moment later, Madame Peeters was talking French.

'You'll find them in the drawing room . . .'

'What is it, Machère?'

'The . . . There are a couple of things in particular that I'd like to say to you . . .'

'About what?'

'About . . .'

He hesitated to speak, and made gestures of complicity that everyone understood.

'Don't be shy.'

'It's the bargeman . . .'

'Did he come back?'

'No . . . he . . .'

'He's made a confession?'

Machère was in torment. He had come to deliver a piece of information that he saw as being of the greatest importance and which he wanted to keep secret and he was having to talk in front of four people!

'He . . . They found his cap and his jacket . . .'

'The old one or the new one?'

'I don't understand.'

'Was it his Sunday jacket, the blue woollen cloth one, that they found?'

'Blue woollen cloth, yes . . . on the shore . . .'

Everyone fell silent. Anna, who was standing up, looked

at the inspector without so much as a twitch. Joseph Peeters stroked his hands with annoyance.

'Go on!'

'He must have thrown himself into the Meuse . . . His cap was fished out near the barge just behind his . . . The barge stopped it . . . You understand?'

'And then?'

'His jacket was on the shore . . . And there was this piece of paper pinned to it . . .'

He took it carefully out of his wallet. It was a shapeless piece of paper, drenched by the rain. It was still just about possible to read:

I'm a wretch. I'd prefer the river . . .

Maigret had read under his breath. Joseph Peeters asked in a troubled voice:

'I don't understand . . . What does he mean?'

Machère stayed standing, unsettled, uneasy. Marguerite looked at each of them in turn with big, inexpressive eyes.

'I think you're the one who . . .' Machère began.

And Maigret got up cordially, with a hearty smile on his lips. He reserved his special attention for Anna.

'You see! I was talking to you about a hammer a moment ago . . .'

'Don't!' begged Marguerite.

'What are you doing tomorrow afternoon?'

'The same as every Sunday . . . We spend it with the family . . . Only Maria will be missing . . .'

'Will you let me come and pay my compliments?

Perhaps there might be some of that excellent rice tart . . . ?'

And Maigret made for the corridor, where he put on his overcoat, made twice as heavy by the rain.

'Please excuse me . . .' stammered Machère. 'It was the inspector who wanted . . .'

'Come!'

In the shop, Madame Peeters had hoisted herself on to a ladder to take down a packet of starch from the top shelf. A bargeman's wife was waiting with a gloomy expression, with a string shopping bag on her arm.

8. The Visit to the Ursulines

There was a little group of people near the place where the sailor's cap had been fished out, but Maigret, dragging Machère with him, walked towards the bridge.

'You hadn't told me about this hammer . . . If you had, I'd have known . . .'

'What have you been doing all day?'

And Machère looked like a schoolboy who had been caught out.

'I went to Namur . . . I wanted to check that Maria Peeters' sprain . . .'

'Well?'

'They wouldn't let me in . . . I ended up in a convent full of nuns looking at me like a beetle that had fallen into their soup . . .'

'Did you insist?'

'I even used threats.'

Maigret suppressed a smile of amusement. Near the bridge, he went into a garage that hired cars and asked for a car and driver to take him to Namur.

Fifty kilometres there and fifty kilometres back, along the Meuse.

'Will you come with me?'

'Do you want me to . . . ? Because I tell you, they won't

let you in . . . Not to mention that now they've found the hammer . . .'

'Fine! Do something else. You take a car as well. Go to all the little stations in a twenty-kilometre radius. Check that the bargeman hasn't taken the train . . .'

And Maigret's car set off. Snug in the cushions, the inspector smoked his pipe beatifically; all that he saw of the landscape was the starburst of lights on each side of the car.

He knew that Maria Peeters was a form mistress in a school run by the Ursulines. He also knew that the Ursulines are, in the religious hierarchy, the equivalent of the Jesuits, which is to say that in a sense they form its teaching aristocracy. The cream of the province must have sent their children to the school in Namur.

Given that, it was amusing to imagine Inspector Machère in discussion with the nuns, insisting on getting inside and even using threats!

'I forgot to ask him what he called them . . .' Maigret reflected. 'He must have said *ladies* . . . Or even *sister* . . .'

Maigret was big, heavy, wide-shouldered, coarse-featured. And yet, when he rang at the door of the convent, in a little provincial street where grass grew between the cobbles, the lay sister who opened the door to him wasn't startled in the slightest.

'I would like to talk to the Mother Superior!' he said.

'She's in chapel. But once benediction is finished . . .'

And he was brought into a parlour compared to which

the Peeters' dining room was all dirt and chaos. You really could see your face in this parquet floor. You got the sense that not even the slightest thing had changed, that the chairs had stood in the same place for years, that the clock on the mantelpiece had never stopped, had never been fast or slow.

In the sumptuously tiled corridors, sliding footsteps, sometimes whispers. At last, very soft and far away, the sound of an organ playing.

The people at the Quai des Orfèvres would probably have been surprised to see a Maigret very much at his ease. When the Mother Superior came in, he greeted her discreetly, calling her by the name that one must give to the Ursulines, namely:

'Reverend Mother . . .'

She waited, hands on her hips.

'Sorry to disturb you, but I'd like to ask your permission to visit one of your teachers . . . I know the rules forbid it . . . Nonetheless a person's life – or at least their liberty – depends on it . . .'

'Are you from the police as well?'

'I think you received a visit from an inspector?'

'A gentleman who said he was from the police, who made some noise and left shouting that we'd be hearing from him again . . .'

Maigret apologized for him, remained calm, polite and deferential. He uttered a few deft phrases, and a short time later a lay sister was instructed to tell Maria Peeters that there was someone to see her.

'A girl of great merit, I think, Reverend Mother?'

'I have only the very best things to say of her. At first the chaplain and I didn't want to take her because of her parents' trade . . . Not the grocery . . . But the fact that they serve drink . . . We passed over that, and we can only congratulate ourselves . . . Yesterday, coming down the stairs, she twisted her ankle, and since then she's been in bed, very downcast, because she knows it's causing us trouble . . .'

The lay sister came back at last. Maigret followed her along endless corridors. He met several groups of pupils all dressed in the same way: black dress with little pleats and blue silk ribbon around their necks.

At last, on the second floor, a door opened. The lay sister asked if she should stay or go.

'Leave us, sister . . .'

A very simple little room. Oil-painted walls, decorated with religious lithographs in black frames and a big crucifix.

An iron bed. A thin figure barely visible under the covers.

Maigret couldn't see a face. No one said anything to him. Once the door had closed he stayed motionless for a while, embarrassed by his wet hat, his thick coat.

At last he heard a muffled sob. But Maria Peeters still hid her face in the blankets, and stayed turned towards the wall.

'Don't be upset . . .' he murmured mechanically. 'Your sister Anna must have told you that I come as a friend . . .'

But that did nothing to calm the girl. On the contrary! Her body was agitated now by real nervous spasms.

'What did the doctor say? Are you to stay in bed for a long time?'

It was awkward, talking to an invisible person like that. Particularly given that Maigret didn't even know her!

The sobs came less quickly. She must have been regaining her composure. She sniffed, and her hand looked for a handkerchief under the pillow.

'Why are you so nervous? The Mother Superior was just telling me how highly she thinks of you!'

'Leave me alone!' she pleaded.

And at that moment there was a knock on the door, and the Mother Superior came in as if she had been waiting for the moment to intervene.

'Sorry! I know that our poor, sensitive Maria . . .'

'Has she always been like this?'

'She is a delicate character . . . When she knew that her sprain was going to immobilize her, and that she wouldn't be able to take a class for at least a week, she fell into despair . . . Show us your face, Maria . . .'

And the girl shook her head in vehement denial.

'We know, of course,' the Mother Superior continued, 'about the accusations that people are making about her family. I have held three masses that the truth may soon emerge . . . I've just been praying for you again at benediction, Maria . . .'

At last she showed her face. A thin little face, very pale, with red marks produced by fever and tears.

She didn't look at all like Anna, but more like her mother, having inherited her features, fine but unfortunately so irregular that she could not pass for pretty.

Her nose was too long and pointed, her lips wide and thin.

'Please forgive me!' she said, dabbing her eyes with her handkerchief. 'I'm too nervous . . . To think I've been lying here while . . . Are you Detective Chief Inspector Maigret? Have you seen my brother?'

'I left him less than an hour ago. He was at your house, with Anna and your cousin Marguerite . . .'

'How is he?'

'Very calm . . . He's confident . . .'

Was she going to start crying again? The Mother Superior encouraged Maigret with a look. She was happy to see him talking like that, with a calm authority that could only make a favourable impression on an invalid.

'Anna told me you had decided to take the veil . . .'

Maria was crying again. She didn't even try to hide it. She took no interest in her appearance and showed her face, glistening and swollen.

'It's a decision we've been waiting for her to take for a long time,' the Mother Superior murmured. 'Maria belongs more to religion than to the world . . .'

Her fit began again, the sobbing burst painfully from her slender throat. And her body was still agitated, her hands clutching the covers.

'You see that I did the right thing, earlier, not to let that gentleman up!' the nun said in a low voice.

Maigret was still standing up, in his overcoat, which made him even bulkier. He looked at the bed and that girl in such a state.

'Has the doctor seen her?'

'Yes . . . He says the sprain is nothing . . . The most serious thing is the fit of nerves that came after it . . . Do you think we should leave her alone? Calm down, Maria . . . I'm going to send Mother Julienne, who will stay close to you . . .'

The last image that Maigret caught was the whiteness of the bed, the sparse hair on the pillow and an eye that stared at him as he walked backwards towards the door.

In the corridor, the Mother Superior spoke quietly as she slipped along the waxed floor.

'She has never enjoyed very good health . . . This scandal has taken its toll on her nerves, and I'm sure it's because of her agitation that she fell down the stairs . . . She's ashamed for her brother, for her family . . . She has told me several times that after that the order won't allow her in . . . For hours at a time she remains prostrate, staring at the ceiling, without taking the slightest nourishment . . . Then, for no apparent reason, another fit will break out . . . We're giving her injections to try to restore her . . .'

They had reached the ground floor.

'Can I ask you what you think of this business, inspector?'

'You can, but I would be embarrassed to give you an answer . . . In all conscience, I must tell you that I don't know anything . . . Not until tomorrow . . .'

'You think that tomorrow . . . ?'

'All I can do, Reverend Mother, is thank you and apologize for this visit . . . Perhaps I might take the liberty of phoning you to ask you for news?'

At last he was outside. He was breathing fresh air,

saturated with rain. He found his taxi waiting beside the pavement.

'To Givet!'

He stuffed his pipe to the brim and almost lay down at the back of the car. At a turn in the road, near Dinant, he spotted a signpost:

Rochefort Caves . . .

He had no time to read the number of kilometres. He only looked into the darkness of a side road. And he imagined a fine Sunday, a train full of tourists, two couples: Joseph Peeters and Germaine Piedboeuf . . . And Anna and Gérard . . .

It must have been hot . . . On the way back, the travellers probably had their arms full of wild flowers . . .

Anna on the bench, wounded, emotional, upset, perhaps watching the expression of the man who had just changed her whole being . . . ?

And Gérard, very cheerful, playful, cracking jokes, unable to understand that a serious, almost defining event had taken place that afternoon . . .

Had he tried to see her again? Had the affair continued?

'No!' Maigret replied to himself. 'Anna understood! She had no illusions about her companion! The very next day, she must have avoided him . . .'

And he imagined her keeping her secret, perhaps fearing for months the consequences of that embrace, and nurturing for men, for all men, a wild hatred.

'Do you want me to drive you to your hotel?'

Already at Givet, the Belgian border and its guard in khaki, the French border, the barges, the Flemish house, the muddy quay.

Maigret was surprised to find something heavy in his pocket. He plunged his hand in, and found the hammer, which he had stopped thinking about.

Inspector Machère, who had heard the car stopping, was in the doorway of the café and watched Maigret paying the driver.

'Did they let you in?'

'Of course!'

'I'm amazed! Because if you want to know what I think, I'll tell you I was sure she wasn't there . . .'

'Where would she have been?'

'I don't know . . . I don't understand any more . . . Particularly since the hammer . . . Do you know who came to see me?'

'The bargeman?'

And Maigret, who had come into the café, ordered a beer and sat down in the corner near the window.

'Almost! In the end, it's more or less the same thing . . . It was Gérard Piedboeuf who came . . . I had driven around all the stations . . . I hadn't found anything . . .'

'And did he reveal your man's hiding place?'

'He told me, at any rate, that he'd been seen taking the 4.15 train at Givet station . . . That's the train that goes to Brussels . . .'

'Who saw him?'

'A friend of Gérard . . . He suggested bringing him to me . . .'

'Shall I lay two places?' asked the landlord.

'Yes . . . No . . . It doesn't matter . . .'

Maigret greedily drank his beer.

'Is that all?'

'Don't you think it's enough? If he really was seen at the station, it means he isn't dead . . . And especially that he's on the run . . . If he is on the run . . .'

'Obviously!'

'You think the same thing as I do!'

'I don't think anything at all, Machère! I'm hot! I'm freezing! I think I've caught a bad cold . . . Right now, I'm dithering over whether I'm going to go to bed without eating . . . Another beer, please! . . . In fact, no! A hot toddy . . . With lots of rum . . .'

'Did she really have a sprain?'

Maigret didn't reply. He was gloomy. One might almost have said that he was worried.

'I suppose the examining magistrate must have given you a blank arrest warrant?'

'Yes . . . But he advised me to be very prudent, because of the mentality in small towns. I'd rather phone him before doing anything definitive.'

'And what are you going to do?'

'I've already sent a telegram to the criminal investigations department in Brussels, to arrest the sailor when he gets off the train. I'll have to ask you to give me back the hammer.'

To the great surprise of the few customers, Maigret took the object out of his pocket and put it on the marble tabletop.

'Is that all?'

'You'll also have to hand it in, because you're the one who found it.'

'Not at all! Not at all! As far as everyone's concerned, you're the one who found it.'

Machère's eyes shone with joy.

'Thank you. It's valuable for my promotion.'

'I've laid two places near the stove!' the landlord announced.

'Thank you! I'm going to bed! I'm not hungry . . .'

And Maigret went up to his room, after shaking his colleague's hand.

Perhaps he had caught a cold by walking around for two days wearing damp clothes, because he hadn't brought his spare suit.

He lay down like a man exhausted. For a good half hour he struggled against the vague images that passed across his retina in a wearying cadence.

However, on Sunday morning he was the first one up. In the café, he found only the waiter who was lighting the percolator, filling the upper part with ground coffee.

The town was still asleep. Dawn was just succeeding night, and the street lamps were still lit.

On the river, on the other hand, they were calling from one barge to another, they were throwing cables, and a tug moved to the head of the line.

A new train of boats set off towards Belgium and Holland.

It wasn't raining. But the fog left droplets of water on his shoulders.

The bells of a church were ringing, somewhere. A light at a window in the Flemish house. Then the door opening up. Madame Peeters closing it carefully again and leaving on hasty feet, clutching a missal wrapped in cloth.

Maigret spent the whole morning outside, just occasionally going into a café to have a glass of alcohol and warm himself up. People who knew said it was going to freeze, and that it would be a disaster for the regions flooded when the river broke its banks.

At half past seven, Madame Peeters, back from mass, drew back the shutters of the shop and, in the kitchen, lit her fire.

It was not until about nine o'clock that Joseph appeared in the doorway for a moment, without a false collar, not yet washed or shaved, his hair dishevelled.

At ten o'clock, he set off for mass with Anna, who was wearing a new beige woollen coat.

At the Café des Mariniers, they didn't yet know whether a tug whose arrival they were expecting would agree to leave the same day with a train of boats, so the bargemen were there all day, occasionally popping outside to look at the swollen river.

It was nearly midday when Gérard Piedboeuf came out of his house, in his Sunday suit, wearing yellow shoes, a light-coloured felt hat and gloves. He passed very close by Maigret. His first thought was not to talk to him, not even to greet him.

But he couldn't resist his desire to show off, or reveal the depths of his thoughts.

'I bother you, don't I? How you must hate me!'

He had circles under his eyes. Since his angry outburst in the Café de la Mairie, he had been living in a state of anxiety.

Maigret shrugged and turned his back on him. And he saw the midwife putting the child in a pram and pushing it towards the centre of town.

There was no sign of Machère. It was only shortly before one o'clock that Maigret met him, at the Café de la Mairie, in fact. Gérard was at another table, with his two companions and his friend from the other evening.

As for Machère, he was surrounded by three men whom the inspector thought he had seen before.

'The deputy mayor . . . The chief inspector of police . . . His secretary . . .' said Machère by way of introduction.

They were all in their Sunday suits and drinking pastis. Judging by the saucers on the table, they had had three drinks each. Machère seemed unusually confident.

'I was telling these gentlemen that the investigation is nearly over . . . Now it depends mostly on the Belgian police . . . I'm surprised I haven't yet had a telegram from Brussels telling me that the bargeman has been arrested . . .'

'They don't deliver telegrams on Sundays after eleven o'clock in the morning!' said the deputy mayor. 'Unless you go to the post office in person . . . What can we get you, Detective Chief Inspector? Did you know that people have been talking about you a lot around here?'

'I'm delighted!'

'I mean they've been saying bad things. They see your attitude as . . .'

'A beer, please! Make it a cold one!'

'You drink beer at this time of day?'

Marguerite was passing along the street, and you could tell by her bearing that she was the elegant young woman of the town and that she knew all eyes were on her.

'What's annoying is that these sex crimes . . . Heavens! There haven't been any in Givet for ten years . . . Last time, it was a Polish workman who . . .'

'You'll forgive me, gentlemen . . .'

And Maigret hurried outside and in the main street he met Anna Peeters and her brother, who were walking with their heads held high, as if to defy suspicion.

'I would like to come and see you this afternoon, as I said I would yesterday . . .'

'At about what time?'

'Half past three . . . Does that suit?'

And he came back all alone, looking grumpy, to his hotel, where he ate at an isolated table.

'Get me Paris on the phone.'

'It doesn't work after eleven o'clock on Sundays.'

'Too bad!'

As he had his lunch, he read a little local newspaper, and a headline amused him:

The Mystery of Givet Deepens

For him, there was no mystery.

'Bring me some beans!' he called to the waiter.

9. Around a Wicker Armchair

Of all the little Sunday family rituals, the one that struck Maigret the most was their carrying old Peeters' wicker armchair from the kitchen to the drawing room.

In the week, the place of the armchair, and consequently of the old man, was beside the stove. Even if they were receiving people in the dining room, old Peeters didn't appear.

But there was a Sunday place, near the window overlooking the courtyard. The meerschaum pipe with its long cherry-wood stem was on the window-sill, near a jar of tobacco.

In a smaller armchair, a leather one, in front of the coalnut fire, Dr Van de Weert sat with his chubby legs crossed.

As he read the report from the Belgian legal doctor, he constantly nodded, with approval, with amazement, making tiny gestures to himself.

At last he held out the report to Maigret. Marguerite, who was between them, tried to take it.

'No! Not you . . .' Van de Weert broke in.

'I'm sure you'll be more interested in this!' Maigret said, passing the pages to Joseph Peeters.

They were all around the table: Joseph and Marguerite, Anna and her mother, who got up every now and again to check on the coffee.

In the Belgian way, the doctor was drinking Burgundy and smoking a cigar, whose lit end he constantly waved about under his chin.

On the kitchen table, Maigret had seen half a dozen tarts.

'A good report, obviously . . . For example, it doesn't say whether . . . whether . . .'

He looked at his daughter with embarrassment.

'You understand what I mean . . . it doesn't say whether . . .'

'Whether there was a rape!' Maigret said abruptly.

And he nearly burst out laughing at the sight of the scandalized face of the doctor, who didn't imagine that such words could be uttered.

'It would have been interesting to know, because in similar cases . . . For example, in 1911 . . .'

He went on talking, telling, with respectable euphemisms, the story of some affair or other. But Maigret wasn't listening. He was watching Joseph Peeters read the document.

Now in the bluntest terms it gave a minute description of the corpse of Germaine Piedboeuf when it was pulled from the Meuse.

Joseph was pale. He had pinched nostrils, something he had in common with his sister Maria.

It looked as if he was about to stop reading and give the papers to Maigret. But it didn't happen. He carried on to the end. As he turned the page, Anna, who had been leaning over his shoulder, halted him:

'Wait . . .'

She had another three lines to read. Then together they both started the following page, which began with:

> ... the wound in the cranium was such that it has been impossible to find the slightest trace of brain ...

'Would you take your glass, inspector? I'm about to lay the table . . .'

And Madame Peeters set down the ashtray, the cigars and the bottle of genever on the mantelpiece, and spread a hand-embroidered cloth on the table.

Her children were still reading. Marguerite looked at them enviously. As for the doctor, he had noticed that no one was listening to him and was smoking in silence.

At the end of the second page, Joseph Peeters was pale, with a dark hollow on each side of his nose and perspiration on his temples. He forgot to turn the page and Anna had to do it, before reading on to the end alone.

Marguerite took the opportunity to get up and touch the young man's shoulder.

'Poor Joseph! You shouldn't have . . . Believe me. Go and get a breath of fresh air . . .'

Maigret saw an opportunity.

'That's an idea! I need to stretch my legs too . . .'

A little later they were both on the quay, bareheaded. It had stopped raining. A few anglers were making use of the tiniest free spaces between the barges. From the other side of the bridge there came the constant noise of a cinema.

Nervously, Peeters lit a cigarette, gazing vacantly at the receding surface of the water.

'It does something to you, doesn't it? . . . Forgive my question . . . Do you still expect to marry Marguerite?'

The silence lasted for a long time. Joseph avoided turning towards Maigret, who could only see his profile. At last he looked at the shop door, decorated with transparent advertisements, then the bridge, then the Meuse again.

'I don't know . . .'

'But you loved her . . .'

'Why did you make me read that report?'

And he ran his hand over his forehead. When he took it back it was wet, in spite of the cold air.

'Was Germaine much less pretty?'

'Be quiet . . . I don't know . . . I've heard it said so often that Marguerite is beautiful, that she's fine, intelligent, well brought-up . . .'

'And now?'

'I don't know . . .'

He didn't want to speak. He only articulated the words reluctantly, because he couldn't fall completely silent. He had torn the paper of his cigarette.

'Has she agreed to get married, in spite of your son?'

'She wants to adopt him.'

His features didn't move. But he seemed ill with disgust, or with weariness. He observed Maigret from the corner of his eye, afraid that he might start asking him new questions.

'Everyone seems to think there's a wedding on the way. Is Marguerite your lover?'

He muttered, in a very low voice:

'No.'

'Didn't she want to?'

'It wasn't her, it was me . . . I didn't even think about it . . . You can't possibly understand . . .'

And suddenly, in a furious voice:

'I have to marry her! I have to, and that's all there is to it!'

The two men still weren't looking at each other. Maigret, who didn't have his overcoat with him, started to feel the cold.

At that moment the door to the shop opened. There was the sound of the bell, familiar to Maigret. Then Marguerite's voice, too sweet, too caressing.

'Joseph! What are you doing?'

Peeters' eyes met Maigret's. It was almost as if he was saying, 'That's all there is to it!'

While Marguerite went on:

'You're going to catch cold . . . Everyone's sitting at the table . . . What's wrong? You're pale . . .'

A pause, to look at the corner of the little street where, invisible from the grocery, the Piedboeufs' house stood.

Anna sliced the tarts.

Madame Peeters didn't speak much, as if she had realized her inferiority. On the other hand, as soon as one of her children spoke, she showed her approval by smiling or nodding her head.

'You'll forgive my indiscretion, inspector . . . I may be about to say something stupid . . .'

And she set down a big slice of rice tart on Maigret's plate.

'I . . . I heard they'd found some things on board the *Étoile Polaire*, and that the bargeman was on the run . . . He came here a few times . . . I had to throw him out, first because he wanted everything on credit, then because he was drunk from dawn till dusk . . . But that's not what I wanted to say . . . If he's on the run, it's because he's guilty . . . And in that case the investigation's over, isn't it?'

Anna ate indifferently, without looking at Maigret. Marguerite said to Joseph:

'A small piece . . . Please! Do it for me . . .'

And Maigret, with his mouth full, spoke to Madame Peeters:

'I could tell you if I was in charge of the inquiry, which isn't the case . . . Don't forget that it's your daughter who asked me to come here to try and prove your innocence . . .'

Van de Weert was restless in his chair, like a man who wants to speak and who isn't allowed to get a word in edgeways.

'But in the end . . .'

'Inspector Machère remains master of the situation.'

'But in the end, detective chief inspector, there is a hierarchy . . . He's just an inspector and you are . . .'

'Here I'm nothing . . . Look! If I were to question one of you, you would have the right not to reply. I went on board the barge because the bargeman wanted me to . . . It was chance that led me to discover the crime weapon, as well as the little coat that the victim wore . . .'

'But . . .'

'But nothing! We're going to try to arrest the man. It may even have happened by now! Except that he's capable of defending himself. For example, he might say that he found that piece of clothing and that hammer, and that he kept them without knowing what they represented . . . He might also say that he fled because he was frightened. He's already had some run-ins with the law. He knows it'll be harder for him to be believed than it will for someone else . . .'

'That doesn't hold water!'

'An accusation hardly ever holds water, any more than the defence. Other people might be accused . . . Do you know what I found out this afternoon? That Gérard, Germaine's brother, hasn't known for a month how he'll get out of the fix he finds himself in . . . He has debts everywhere . . . Worse than that! He was persuaded to take money from the till and, until the sum has been paid back, half his wages are being held back every month . . .'

'Really?'

'But to go from there to saying that he had his sister killed to get the damages . . .'

'It would be appalling!' sighed Madame Peeters, who was put off her food by the conversation.

'You knew him quite well, didn't you?' said Maigret turning towards Joseph.

'I used to spend a bit of time with him a long time ago . . .'

'Before the birth of the child, isn't that right? You went on outings together a number of times . . . If I'm not mistaken, your sister even went with you to the caves at . . .'

'Really?' said Madame Peeters with astonishment, turning towards her daughter. 'I didn't know that.'

'I don't remember!' said Anna, who had gone on eating, and whose eyes were fixed on the inspector.

'It doesn't matter, anyway . . . But what was I saying? Would you please pass me a slice of tart, Mademoiselle Anna? No, not with fruit . . . I'm staying true to your magnificent rice tart . . . Did you make it yourself?'

'She did!' her mother asserted hastily.

And silence fell suddenly, because Maigret wasn't saying anything, and no one dared to speak. The sound of chewing could be heard. The inspector dropped his fork on the ground and had to bend down to pick it up. As he did so, he saw that Marguerite's finely shod foot was resting on Joseph's.

'Inspector Machère is a resourceful chap!'

'He doesn't seem very clever!' Anna articulated slowly.

And Maigret gave her a complicit smile.

'So few people look intelligent! For example, if I'm in the presence of a possible culprit, I make a point of acting like an imbecile . . .'

It was the first time that Maigret had spoken in a way that might have seemed confidential.

'Your forehead can't change!' Doctor Van de Weert hurried to declare politely. 'And, for someone who's done a little phrenology . . . For example, I'm sure you have a terrible temper . . .'

Lunch was coming to an end at last. The inspector was the first to push his chair back. He then picked up his pipe, which he set about filling.

'Do you know what you should do, Mademoiselle Marguerite? Sit down at the piano and play us "Solveig's Song" . . .'

She hesitated and looked at Joseph, seeking his advice, while Madame Peeters murmured:

'She plays so well! And she sings!'

'There's only one thing I regret: it's that Mademoiselle Maria's sprain stops her from being with us . . . For my last day . . .'

Anna quickly turned her head in his direction.

'Are you leaving soon?'

'This evening . . . I'm not a man of leisure . . . Besides, I'm married, and my wife's getting impatient . . .'

'And Inspector Machère?'

'I don't know what he'll decide . . . I suppose . . .'

The shop bell rang. There were hurried steps, then knocking at the door.

It was Machère himself, very agitated.

'Is the detective chief inspector here?'

He hadn't seen him straight away, surprised to find himself in the middle of a family reunion.

'What is it?'

'I need to talk to you.'

'Will you excuse me?'

And he went with Machère to the shop, where he leaned on the counter.

*

'How I loathe those people!'

Machère, on edge, jutted his chin towards the dining-room door.

'Just the smell of their coffee and their tart . . .'

'Is that what you wanted to tell me?'

'No! I've got news from Brussels . . . The train arrived on time . . .'

'But the bargeman wasn't on it!'

'You knew that?'

'I suspected as much! Did you think he was an idiot? I didn't. He must have got off at a little station somewhere and caught another train and then another . . . Tonight he could be in Germany, perhaps in Amsterdam, perhaps even in Paris . . .'

But Machère looked at him with a chuckle.

'If he had any money!'

'What do you mean?'

'That I've made my inquiries. The man's name is Cassin. Yesterday morning he couldn't settle his bill in the bistro, and they refused to serve him . . . Better than that! He owed money to everybody . . . To the point that the shopkeepers had decided not to let him leave on his boat . . .'

Maigret looked at his companion with total indifference.

'And?'

'I didn't stop there. And it was hard, because it's Sunday, and most people aren't at home . . . I went all the way to the cinema to question certain people . . .'

Maigret, smoking his pipe, was amusing himself by putting weights on both trays of the scales, trying to make them balance.

'I discovered that Gérard Piedboeuf borrowed 2,000 francs, yesterday, giving as guarantee his father's signature, because no one wanted his . . .'

'Did they meet?'

'Indeed! A customs man saw Gérard Piedboeuf and Cassin walking along the bank together, over by Belgian customs . . .'

'What time was it?'

'Just after two . . .'

'That's perfect!'

'What's perfect? If Piedboeuf gave money to the bargeman . . .'

'Beware of leaping to conclusions, Machère! It's very dangerous to try to conclude . . .'

'Nevertheless, the man, who hadn't a penny to his name in the morning, left by train in the afternoon, with money in his pocket. I went to the station. He bought his ticket with a thousand-franc note . . . Apparently he had more . . .'

'Or *one* more?'

'Maybe more, maybe one more . . . What would you do in my position?'

'Me?'

'Yes.'

Maigret sighed, knocked his pipe against his heel to empty it and pointed to the dining-room door:

'I'd come and get a good glass of genever . . . Particularly if someone was going to play us a piece on the piano!'

'That's all that . . .'

'Let's go! Come on . . . You have nothing more to do in town at this hour of day . . . Where's Gérard Piedboeuf?'

'At the Scala cinema, with a girl from the factory.'

'I bet they've taken a box!'

And Maigret, with a silent laugh, pushed his colleague towards the drawing room, where dusk was beginning to blur the outlines of things. A wisp of smoke rose slowly from Van de Weert's armchair. Madame Peeters was in the kitchen, doing the washing-up. Marguerite, at the piano, was nonchalantly moving her fingers back and forth on the keys.

'You really want me to play?'

'I'd love you to . . . Sit here, Machère . . .'

Joseph was standing up, his elbow resting on the mantelpiece, his eye fixed on the grimy window.

Winter may flee
Beloved spring
May pass
The autumn leaves
And the fruits of summer
Everything may pass . . .

Her voice lacked firmness. Marguerite struggled to reach the top notes. Twice she missed her chords.

But you will return to me,
O my handsome betrothed,
Never again to leave me . . .

★

Anna wasn't there any more. She wasn't in the kitchen, where Madame Peeters could be heard coming and going, making as little noise as possible out of respect for the music.

. . . I gave you my heart . . .

Marguerite couldn't see the gloomy figure of Joseph, who had let his cigarette go out.

Now that night was falling, the coal-nut fire cast a purple glow on the room, particularly the painted feet of the table.

To the great amazement of Machère, who didn't dare move, Maigret left so discreetly that no one noticed. He climbed the stairs without making a single step creak and found himself in front of two closed doors.

The landing was already in almost complete darkness. Only the doorknobs, being made of porcelain, appeared as two milky patches.

At last the chief inspector put his pipe, still lit, in his pocket, turned one of the doorknobs, went inside and closed the door behind him.

Anna was there. Because of the curtains, the room was darker than the dining room. There was a kind of grey dust floating in the air, denser in the corners.

Anna didn't move. Hadn't she heard anything?

She was at the window, against the light, her face turned towards the twilit landscape of the Meuse. On the opposite shore, lights had been lit, which cast bright rays into the chiaroscuro.

From behind, it looked as if Anna was crying. She was tall. She looked more vigorous, more of a 'statue' than ever.

And her grey dress actually seemed to fade into the background.

A floorboard, just one, creaked when Maigret was no more than a foot from the girl, but it didn't make her start.

Then he put his hand on her shoulder, with surprising gentleness, sighing like a man who can finally allow himself to speak in confidence:

'So here we are!'

She turned towards him, all at once. She was calm. Not a wrinkle broke the severe harmony of her features.

Nothing but her throat, which swelled slightly, slowly, under a mysterious inner pressure . . .

The notes of the piano reached them clearly, and they could hear all the syllables of 'Solveig's Song'.

> May God in his great goodness
> Protect you still . . .

And two clear eyes sought Maigret's eyes, while lips that had almost parted in a sob stiffened like the rest of Anna's body.

10. Solveig's Song

'What are you doing here?'

Strangely, the tone wasn't aggressive. Anna looked at Maigret with annoyance, perhaps with horror, but not with hatred.

'You heard what I said just now. I'm leaving this evening. We have been living in very close proximity for some days.'

And he looked around at the two girls' bed, the polar-bear skin that they used as a rug, the wallpaper with little pink flowers, the mirrored wardrobe that now reflected only the shadows of night.

'I didn't want to leave without having one last conversation with you . . .'

The rectangle of the window formed something like a screen on which the figure of Anna appeared, less resolute with each passing minute. And Maigret spotted a detail that he hadn't noticed before. An hour before, he couldn't have said how her hair was done. He knew now. Her long hair, tightly braided, rested against the back of her neck in a heavy coil.

'Anna!' cried Madame Peeters' voice in the corridor below.

The piano had fallen silent. The disappearance of the two people had been noticed.

'Yes! I'm here . . .'

'Have you seen Inspector Maigret?'

'Yes! We're coming down . . .'

To answer, she had walked towards the door. She came back towards her companion, very serious, her expression dramatically steadfast.

'What do you have to say to me?'

'You know!'

She didn't look away. She went on looking at him ardently, her hands folded over her belly in a pose that was already that of an old woman.

'What are you going to do?'

'I told you: go back to Paris . . .'

Then, however, her voice thickened.

'What about me?'

It was the first time he had ever been aware of an emotion in her. She was aware of it herself. And, probably to help herself overcome her unease, she walked to the light switch and turned it on.

The light had a yellow silk shade and lit only a circle two metres in diameter on the floor.

'First of all I have to ask you a question!' said Maigret. 'Who provided the money? You had to move fast, didn't you, to put funds together in a few minutes. The bank was shut. I'm sure you don't keep large amounts of money in the house. You haven't got a telephone . . .'

It was slow. The silence around them was unusually intense.

And Maigret went on breathing in that quiet, lower-middle-class atmosphere. There was a faint murmur of voices below, Dr Van de Weert stretching his short legs towards the stove, Joseph and Marguerite looking at each other in silence. Machère, who must have been getting impatient, and Madame Peeters picking up some embroidery or filling glasses of genever.

But Maigret kept finding Anna's clear eyes, and she finally spoke:

'It's Marguerite . . .'

'Did she have money at her house?'

'Money and shares. She herself takes care of the share of the fortune left to her by her mother.'

And Anna repeated:

'What are you going to do?'

As she said that her eyes moistened, but it was so brief that Maigret thought he might have been mistaken.

'And you?'

The fact that this question constantly came back proved that they were both afraid of broaching the main topic.

'How did you lure Germaine Piedboeuf into your room? Wait! Don't tell me straight away . . . She came of her own accord that evening, to ask about Joseph and claim the child's money . . . Your mother let her in . . . You came into the shop as well . . . Did you know that you were going to kill her?'

'Yes!'

No more emotion, panic. A clear voice.

'For how long?'

'About a month.'

And Maigret sat down on the edge of the bed, the girls' bed, Anna and Maria's bed, ran his hand over his forehead as he looked at the wallpaper that served as a backdrop to his adversary.

Now she looked as if she was proud of what she had done. She claimed all responsibility for it. She was proclaiming her premeditation.

'You love your brother as much as that?'

He knew. And it wasn't just Anna. Was it because old Peeters had ceased to be part of the family a long time ago? The three women, at any rate, his mother and his two sisters, held the young man in the same adoration, which almost assumed a certain ambiguity in Anna's case.

He wasn't handsome. He was thin. His features were irregular. His lanky build, his big nose, his eyes with their weary pupils emanated boredom.

He was still a god! And it was as a god that Marguerite loved him!

It was like a case of collective suggestion, and it was easy to imagine the two sisters, the mother and the cousin, spending whole afternoons talking about him . . .

'I didn't want him to kill himself!'

Suddenly, Maigret almost got angry. He leaped to his feet and paced back and forth in the room.

'He said that?'

'If he had had to marry Germaine, he would have killed himself on the evening of their wedding . . .'

He didn't laugh, but he gave a terrible shrug. He remembered Joseph's confidences the other evening! Joseph, who didn't even know who he loved any more! Joseph, who was almost as afraid of Marguerite as he was of Germaine Piedboeuf!

Only, to flatter his sisters, to keep their admiration, he assumed the attitudes of a romantic hero.

'His life was broken . . .'

Good heavens! It all sat very well with 'Solveig's Song'!

> But you will return to me,
> O my handsome betrothed . . .

And they had all bought into it! They had been drugged by music, poetry and confidences.

But what a fine fellow he was, the handsome betrothed, with his ill-cut jackets and short-sighted eyes!

'Did you talk about your plan to anyone?'

'No one!'

'Not even him?'

'Especially not him!'

'And you had had the hammer in your room for a month? Wait! I'm starting to understand!'

He was also starting to breathe violently, because he was being drawn in by both the tragedy and the meanness of the whole affair.

He barely dared to look again at Anna, who didn't move.

'It was important that you weren't caught, isn't that right? Because then Joseph wouldn't have dared to marry Marguerite! You thought of every possible weapon! A revolver would have made too much noise! Since Germaine never ate here, you couldn't use poison . . . If your hands had been strong enough, you would probably have strangled her . . .'

'I thought about it.'

'Shut up, for God's sake! You went and took the hammer from some building site or other, because you aren't stupid enough to take a tool that belonged to the house . . . On what pretext did you persuade Germaine to follow you?'

And she recited indifferently:

'She had been crying, in the shop . . . She was a woman who cried all the time . . . My mother had given her her monthly payment of fifty francs . . . I went outside with her . . . I promised I would give her the rest . . .'

'And you both walked around the house, in the night . . . You came back in by the back door and you went up to the first floor . . .'

He looked at the door, and muttered in what was supposed to be a firm voice:

'You opened the door . . . You let your companion in ahead of you . . . The hammer was ready . . .'

'No!'

'What do you mean, no?'

'I didn't hit her straight away . . . Perhaps I wouldn't have had the courage to hit her . . . I don't know . . . Except that the girl said, looking at the bed: "Is this where my brother comes to see you! You're lucky, you know how to avoid having children!"'

Just a stupid, sordid, mundane detail.

'How many blows?'

'Two . . . She fell straight away . . . I pushed her under the bed . . .'

'And, at the bottom, you found your mother, your sister Maria and Marguerite, who had just arrived . . .'

'My mother was in the kitchen with my father, grinding the coffee for the following morning . . .'

'Now, Anna!' Madame Peeters' voice called again. 'The inspector wants to leave . . .'

And Maigret, leaning over the banister, called out:

'Let him wait!'

He locked the door.

'Did you tell your sister and Marguerite?'

'No! But I knew that Joseph would come. I couldn't do what I had to do on my own. And I didn't want people to see my brother in the house. I told Maria to go and wait on the quay so that he didn't show his face, and that he was to leave his motorbike as far away as possible . . .'

'Was Maria surprised?'

'She was scared. She didn't understand. But she felt that she had to obey . . . Marguerite was at the piano . . . I asked her to play and sing . . . Because I knew we would be making some noise up there . . .'

'And you were the one who came up with the idea of the water-tank on the roof!'

He lit his pipe, which he had filled mechanically.

'Joseph came and joined you in your room. What did he say when he saw . . . ?'

'Nothing! He didn't understand! He looked at me in horror. He was barely able to help me . . .'

'To hoist the body through the skylight and drag it along the cornice to the galvanized tank!'

Big drops of sweat ran down the face of the inspector, who muttered to himself:

'Unbelievable!'

She pretended not to hear.

'If I hadn't killed that woman, Joseph would have died . . .'

'When did you tell the truth to Maria?'

'Never! She didn't dare to ask me . . . When she found out that Germaine had disappeared, she suspected something . . . She's been ill since then . . .'

'And Marguerite?'

'If she has suspicions, she doesn't want to know . . . You understand?'

Did he understand! Madame Peeters continued to come and go in the house without suspecting a thing and was furious about the accusations of the people of Givet!

Old Peeters just went on smoking his pipe in his wicker armchair, where he went to sleep two or three times a day . . .

Joseph appeared as rarely as possible and went back to Nancy, leaving his sister with the task of defending herself.

And Maria was in torment, passing her days at the Ursuline convent with the fear of learning, when she came home one evening, that everything had been discovered.

'Why did you take the body out of the tank?'

'It would have ended up smelling . . . I waited for three days . . . On Saturday, when Joseph came back, we carried it to the Meuse together . . .'

She too had big drops of sweat, but not on her forehead: above her upper lip, exactly where the skin was downy.

'When I saw that the inspector suspected us and was furiously carrying out his investigation, I thought the best way to get people to be quiet was to go to the police myself . . . If they hadn't found the body . . .'

'The case would have been closed!' he muttered.

And he added, starting to walk again:

'Only there was the bargeman, who had seen the body being dumped in the water and who had fished out the hammer and the jacket . . .'

And was he any less cynical than professional criminals? He didn't say anything to the police! Or rather he lied! He let people believe that he knew more than he was willing to admit!

He went and told Gérard Piedboeuf that he could get the Peeters put in jail and, in return for that evidence, he received two thousand francs.

But he didn't give evidence. He spoke to Anna. He told her the deal.

Either she gave him nothing, and he would talk. Or she would give him a lot of money, and he would leave the area, thus drawing suspicion to himself and turning it away from the Flemish house!

It was Marguerite who had paid! They had to get a move on! Maigret had already found the hammer! Anna couldn't leave the grocery without attracting attention! She gave the bargeman a message for her cousin.

And her cousin hurried over a short time later.

'What's happening? Why did you . . . ?'

'Sh! Joseph's coming . . . You'll get married soon . . .'

And the diaphanous Marguerite didn't dare ask anything more.

On Saturday evening there was a relaxed atmosphere in

the house. The danger had been banished. The bargeman was on the run! Now all that mattered was that he didn't get caught!

'And since you feared your sister Maria's nerves,' Maigret growled, 'you advised her to stay in Namur, to say she was sick or give herself a sprain . . .'

He was suffocating. The sound of the piano reached them again, but this time it was playing 'Le Comte de Luxembourg'!

Did Anna realize the monstrousness of her action? She remained absolutely calm. She waited. Her face was still as limpid as before.

'They'll be getting worried down there!' she said.

'You're right! Let's go down . . .'

But she didn't move. She remained standing in the middle of the room, stopping her companion with a gesture.

'What are you going to do?'

'I've told you three times!' Maigret sighed wearily. 'I'm going back to Paris this evening.'

'But . . . the . . .'

'I'm not concerned with the rest! I'm not on duty here. See Inspector Machère . . .'

'Will you tell him?'

He didn't reply. He was already on the landing. He was breathing the mild, sweet smell that spread throughout the whole house, and the dominant hint of cinnamon brought back old memories.

There was a chink of light under the dining-room door. The sound of music could be heard more clearly.

Maigret pushed the door and was surprised to see Anna, whom he hadn't heard, coming in at the same time as he did.

'What have you two been plotting?' asked Dr Van de Weert, who had just lit an enormous cigar and was sucking the end of it like a child sucking on a dummy.

'Excuse us . . . Mademoiselle Anna was asking me for information about a trip that I think she wants to take one of these days . . .'

Marguerite had abruptly stopped playing.

'Is that true, Anna?'

'Oh! Not straight away . . .'

And Madame Peeters, who was knitting, looked at them all with a hint of concern.

'I have filled your glass, inspector . . . I know your tastes now . . .'

Machère, frowning, studied his colleague, trying to guess what had happened.

As for Joseph, he was in high spirits, because he had drunk several glasses of genever in a row. His eyes were shining, his hands agitated.

Maigret said, 'Would you do me the pleasure, Mademoiselle Marguerite? Play me "Solveig's Song" one last time . . .'

And, turning to Joseph:

'Why don't you turn the pages for her?'

It was perversity, as when you prod a diseased tooth with the tip of your tongue in order to provoke the pain.

From the place where he was standing, with one elbow on the mantelpiece, his glass of Schiedam in his hand,

Maigret dominated the whole drawing room, Madame Peeters, leaning over her table and haloed by the light of the lamp, Van de Weert, smoking, stretching his little legs, Anna, still standing against the wall.

And at the piano Marguerite playing and singing, Joseph turning the pages.

The top of the instrument was decorated with a piece of embroidery and lots of photographs: Joseph, Maria and Anna, at all ages . . .

. . . May God in his great goodness . . .

But most of all it was Anna that Maigret was studying. He didn't think he was beaten yet. He was hoping for something, without knowing exactly what.

Genuine emotion, at least! Perhaps a tremor of the lips? Perhaps some tears? Perhaps even a dash out of the room . . .

The first couplet passed with nothing of the kind happening, and Machère murmured in Maigret's ear:

'Are we staying long?'

'A few minutes . . .'

During that brief exchange of words, Anna looked at them over the table, as if to check that no danger was being prepared for her.

. . . Never leave me . . .

And while the last chord was still echoing, Madame Peeters murmured, her white head still bent over her work:

'I've never wished any harm to anyone, but I repeat that God knows what he has to do! Wouldn't it have been miserable if these children . . .'

She was too emotional to finish. She wiped away a tear on her cheek with the stocking she was busy knitting.

And Anna remained impassive, her eyes fixed on Maigret. Machère was getting impatient.

'Right! You'll forgive me for leaving you abruptly, but my train is at seven o'clock and . . .'

Everyone got up. Joseph didn't know where to look. Machère stammered, before finally finding the phrase he was looking for, or something close to it.

'I'm sorry to have suspected you . . . But you must admit that appearances . . . And if that bargeman hadn't gone on the run . . .'

'Will you show these gentlemen out, Anna?'

'Yes, Mother . . .'

So it was just the three of them who crossed the grocery. The door was locked, because it was Sunday. But there was a night light on, making reflections on the brass plates of the scales.

Machère anxiously shook the girl's hand.

'Please accept my apology once again . . .'

Maigret and Anna spent a few seconds standing facing one another, and Anna stammered at last:

'Don't worry . . . I won't be staying here . . .'

In the darkness of the quay, Machère spoke ceaselessly, but Maigret only listened to scraps of what he said.

'. . . as soon as the name of the guilty man is known, I will go back to Nancy tomorrow . . .'

'What did she mean?' Maigret wondered. '"I won't be staying here" . . . Did she really have the courage . . . ?'

He looked at the Meuse, where there was a line of distorted reflections of street lamps at fifty-metre intervals. A brighter light, on the other side of the river, in the yard of the factory where, tonight, old Piedboeuf would bring potatoes that he would cook in the ashes.

They passed by the sidestreet. There was no light on in the house.

11. Anna's Ending

'Did you solve your case?'

Madame Maigret was surprised to see her husband in such a bad mood. She patted the overcoat that she had just helped him take off.

'You've been walking around in the rain again . . . One day you will catch your death, and that will be you done for. And what was this one all about? A crime?'

'A family affair!'

'And the girl who came to see you?'

'A girl! Will you give me my slippers?'

'It's fine! I'm not going to ask you any more questions! Not about this, anyway. Did you eat well in Givet, at least?'

'I don't know . . .'

It was true! He could barely remember the meals he had had.

'Guess what I'm making.'

'Quiches!'

It wasn't hard to guess, given that the whole house smelled of them.

'Are you hungry?'

'Yes, darling . . . At any rate, I'll be hungry soon . . . Tell me what's been going on here . . . Oh, and by the way, that business with the furniture has been sorted out . . .'

Why, when he looked at the dining room, did he always look at the same corner, where there wasn't anything? He didn't realize it himself until his wife said:

'You seem to be looking for something!'

Then, out loud, he exclaimed:

'Good heavens! The piano . . .'

'What piano?'

'Nothing! You wouldn't understand . . . Your quiches are astonishing . . .'

'What's the point of being Alsatian if you don't know how to make quiches? Except if you go on, you won't leave me so much as a slice . . . About pianos, the people on the fourth floor . . .'

A year later, Maigret went into the offices of an import-export company on Rue Poissonnière pursuing a case involving fake bank notes.

The warehouses were enormous, stuffed with goods, but the offices were very small.

'I'll bring you the fake note that I discovered in a bundle . . .' said the boss, pressing down on a stamp.

Maigret looked elsewhere. He vaguely noticed a grey skirt coming towards the desk, legs sheathed in cotton. Then he looked up and stood motionless for a moment looking at the face leaning over the desk.

'Thank you, Mademoiselle Anna . . .'

And as the inspector watched after the office worker, the businessman explained:

'She might look a bit of a dragon . . . But I hope you have a secretary like that one day! She replaces precisely two clerks. She does all the mail and she still has time to do the accounts . . .'

'Have you had her for long?'

'About ten months.'

'Is she married?'

'No! It's her little vice: a mortal hatred that extends to all men . . . One day a colleague who had come to see me tried to pinch her waist as a joke . . . If you'd seen the look he got . . .

'She comes at eight o'clock in the morning, sometimes earlier . . . In the evening she's the one who closes up . . . She must be foreign, because she has a slight accent . . .'

'Can I have a quick word with her?'

'I'll call her.'

'No! I'd like to go to her office and . . .'

And Maigret passed through a glass door. The office looked out on to a yard full of lorries. And the whole company seemed to suffer from the juddering of the flood of buses and cars flowing along Rue Poissonnière.

Anna was calm, as she had been just now when she leaned over her boss, as Maigret had always known her. She must have been twenty-seven, but she looked more like thirty, because her complexion no longer had the same freshness, and her features had faded.

In two or three years, it would be impossible to tell what age she was. In ten years she would be an old woman!

'Have you had any news of your brother?'

She looked away without replying, while mechanically using a rocking blotter.

'Is he married?'

She merely nodded.

'Happily?'

Then the tears for which Maigret had been waiting for such a long time began to pour; at the same time as her throat swelled, and she shouted at him, as if blaming him for everything:

'He's started drinking . . . Marguerite's expecting a baby . . .'

'His business?'

'His chambers didn't bring in anything . . . He had to accept a job at a thousand francs per month, in Reims . . .'

She dabbed her eyes with her handkerchief, little dry, angry blows.

'Maria?

'She died, a week before taking the veil . . .'

The phone rang, and Anna answered it in a different voice, reaching for a notepad:

'Yes, Monsieur Worms . . . of course. Tomorrow evening . . . I'll send a cable right this minute . . . About the cargo of wool, I'll send you a letter containing a few remarks . . . No! I haven't time . . . You'll read it . . .'

She hung up. Her boss was in the doorway, looking at her and Maigret in turn.

The inspector came back into the adjacent office.

'What do you think? And I haven't even mentioned how honest she is. Almost fanatically so . . .'

'Where does she live?'

'I don't know . . . Or rather I don't know her address, but I know it's in a furnished house for women living on their own, kept by some charity or other . . . But . . . Hello!

You're starting to scare me . . . You didn't meet her in the course of your professional duties, did you? Because it would be a bit worrying . . .'

'It wasn't in the course of my professional duties!' Maigret replied slowly. 'So, we were saying that you found that note in a bundle of . . .'

He listened out for the sounds of the adjacent office, where a woman's voice was saying on the telephone:

'No, sir, he's busy! This is Mademoiselle Anna speaking . . . I know about it . . .'

He never heard anything more about the bargeman.

READ ON FOR A PREVIEW OF THE NEXT BOOK
IN THE INSPECTOR MAIGRET SERIES

THE MADMAN OF BERGERAC

1. The Restless Passenger

It all came about by pure chance! The previous day, Maigret had not known that he was about to go on a journey, even though it was the time of year when he usually began to find Paris oppressive. It was a March spiced up with a foretaste of spring and a clear, sharp sun that was already warm.

Madame Maigret was away in Alsace for a couple of weeks, staying with her sister, who was having a baby.

On the Wednesday morning, the inspector received a letter from a former colleague who had retired from the Police Judiciaire two years earlier and moved to the Dordogne.

. . . And of course, if you happen to be in the area, do come and stay with me for a few days. I have an elderly housekeeper who is only too happy when there are guests to fuss over. And it's the start of the salmon season—

Maigret's imagination was particularly fired by the letterhead with its drawing of a manor house flanked by two circular towers above the address:

La Ribaudière
near Villefranche-en-Dordogne

At midday, Madame Maigret telephoned from Alsace to say that her sister would probably give birth that night, adding, 'You'd think it was summer . . . The fruit trees are in blossom!'

Chance . . . Pure chance . . . A little later, Maigret was in the chief's office, chatting, when his superior said, 'By the way . . . Did you ever go to Bordeaux to follow up that matter we talked about?'

It was a minor case of no urgency. At some point, Maigret had to go to Bordeaux to trawl through the municipal records.

One idea led to another: Bordeaux . . . the Dordogne.

At that exact moment, a ray of sunlight struck the crystal globe paperweight on the chief's desk.

'That's a thought! I'm not working on anything at the moment.'

Later that afternoon, having purchased a first-class ticket to Villefranche, Maigret boarded the train at the Gare d'Orsay. The guard reminded him to change trains at Libourne.

'Unless you're in the sleeper compartment which gets hitched to the connecting train.'

Maigret thought no more about it, read a few newspapers and made his way to the dining car where he sat until ten o'clock.

When he returned to his compartment, he found the curtains drawn and the light dimmed. An elderly couple had commandeered both seats.

An attendant walked past.

'Is there a free bunk by any chance?'

'Not in first-class . . . but I think there's one in second . . . If you don't mind—'

'Of course not!'

And Maigret lugged his carpet-bag along the corridors. The attendant opened several doors and finally found the compartment in which only the upper bunk was taken.

Here too, the light was dimmed and the curtains drawn.

'Would you like me to switch on the light?'

'No thank you.'

The air was warm and stuffy. There was a faint hissing sound, as if there was a leak in the radiator pipes. Maigret could hear the person in the top bunk tossing and turning and breathing heavily.

The inspector silently removed his shoes, jacket and waistcoat. He stretched out on the lower bunk and felt a slight draught coming from somewhere. He picked up his bowler hat and put it over his face for protection.

Did he fall asleep? He dozed off, in any case. Perhaps for an hour, perhaps two. Perhaps longer. But he remained half conscious.

And, in that semi-conscious state, he was aware of a feeling of discomfort. Was it because of the heat battling with the draught?

Or was it because of the man in the top bunk, who couldn't keep still for a second? He tossed and turned continually, just above Maigret's head. Every movement made a rustling sound.

His breathing was irregular, as if he had a fever.

After a time, Maigret got up, exasperated, went into

the corridor and paced up and down. But there it was too cold.

So it was back into the compartment, and another attempt to sleep, his thoughts and sensations befuddled by drowsiness.

Cut off from the rest of the world, the atmosphere was that of a nightmare.

Had the man above him just raised himself up on his elbows and leaned over to try and get a look at his companion?

Maigret, meanwhile, didn't dare move. The half-bottle of Bordeaux and the two brandies he had drunk in the dining car lay heavy in his stomach.

The night was long. Whenever the train stopped at a station, there was a babble of voices, footsteps in the corridors, doors slamming. It felt as if the train would never get going again.

It sounded as if the man was crying. There were moments when he held his breath. Then suddenly, there'd be a snivel and he would turn over and blow his nose.

Maigret regretted leaving his first-class compartment occupied by the elderly couple.

He dozed off, woke up and drifted off again. Finally, unable to stand it any longer, he coughed to steady his voice and said, 'Monsieur, would you kindly try to keep still!'

He felt embarrassed, because his voice sounded much sterner than he had intended. Supposing the man was ill?

There was no answer. The tossing and turning stopped. The man must have been making a huge effort to avoid making the slightest sound. And it suddenly occurred to Maigret that it might not be a man after all, but a woman! He hadn't seen the person who was wedged between the bunk and the ceiling.

And the heat must be suffocating up there. Now Maigret tried to turn down the radiator, but the control knob was jammed.

It was three o'clock in the morning.

'I really must get some sleep!'

Now he was wide awake. He had become almost as jumpy as his fellow passenger. He listened out.

'Here we go! He's at it again.'

And Maigret forced himself to breathe regularly and count sheep, in the hope of falling asleep.

The man was definitely crying! Probably someone who had been to Paris for a funeral. Or vice versa, a poor soul who worked in Paris and had received bad news from back home – his mother ill, or dead . . . Or maybe his wife . . . Maigret was sorry he'd been harsh with him. You never knew . . . Sometimes they hitched a special hearse wagon to the train.

His thoughts turned to his sister-in-law in Alsace who was about to give birth. Three children in four years!

Maigret slept.

The train halted, then moved off again. It clattered over an iron bridge, making a terrible racket, and Maigret was suddenly wide awake.

Then he froze at the sight of two legs dangling in front of his nose. The man was sitting on his bunk meticulously lacing up his shoes. It was the first thing that the inspector saw of him and, despite the dim light, he noticed that they were patent-leather shoes. His socks, meanwhile, were grey wool and looked hand-knitted.

The man paused and listened. Had he noticed the change in Maigret's breathing pattern?

Maigret started counting sheep again. It was all the more difficult because he was intrigued by the hands tying the shoelaces. They were trembling so badly that it took the man four attempts to tie the bow.

The train shot through a small station without stopping. All that could be seen through the curtain fabric were the lights flashing past.

The man was coming down! This was slowly turning into a nightmare. Why couldn't he descend in an ordinary fashion? Was he afraid of being rebuked again?

His foot groped for the ladder for ages. He almost tumbled from the bunk. Then, keeping his back to the inspector, the man left the compartment, without bothering to close the door, and headed for the end of the corridor.

Had it not been for the open door, Maigret would probably have turned over and tried to go back to sleep. But he had to get up to shut it. He looked up and down the corridor.

He just had the time to throw on his jacket, not bothering with the waistcoat.

For the stranger had opened the carriage door at the far end of the corridor. It was not by chance: he had opened it just as the train was slowing down.

They were passing a forest. There were a few clouds illuminated by an invisible moon.

The brakes squealed. The train had slowed down from eighty kilometres an hour to around thirty, perhaps even less.

The man jumped off and slipped down the embankment, then vanished in the darkness. Maigret barely stopped to think. He leaped. The train was going even slower now, so he wasn't in any danger.

He landed on his side and rolled over three times, coming to rest by a barbed-wire fence.

The train's red light moved off and the clatter of the wheels grew fainter.

Maigret stood up. He hadn't broken any bones. His companion's fall must have been much harder, for he could see him, fifty metres away, still struggling to get to his feet.

This situation was ridiculous. Maigret wondered what instinct had prompted him to jump off the train while his luggage continued on its way to Villefranche-en-Dordogne. He didn't even know where he was!

He could see nothing but woodland – probably a vast forest. Further away the pale ribbon of a road plunged into the trees.

Why was the man not moving? All Maigret could see was a kneeling shadow. Had he realized he was being followed? Was he hurt?

'Hey! You over there!' shouted Maigret fumbling for the gun in his pocket.

He didn't have time to grab it. He saw a flash of red. And he felt something hit his shoulder even before hearing the report.

The whole thing hadn't lasted a tenth of a second and

already the man had sprung up, sprinted through a copse, crossed the main road and vanished into the pitch darkness.

Maigret cursed. Tears sprang to his eyes, not from the pain, but from shock, rage and confusion. It had all happened so fast! And he was in such a sorry mess!

He dropped his gun, bent down to pick it up and winced because his shoulder hurt.

No, it was something else: the sensation that he was bleeding profusely, that with each heartbeat the warm blood was spurting from a severed artery.

He didn't dare run. He didn't dare move. He didn't even pick up his weapon.

His temples were damp, his throat tight. And, as expected, when he touched his shoulder, his hand came into contact with a sticky liquid. He squeezed and felt for the artery with his fingertips to staunch the flow of blood.

In his semi-conscious state, Maigret had the impression that less than a kilometre away, the train had been stationary for a long, long time while he listened out, acutely anxious.

What could it matter to him if the train had stopped? His response was automatic. The absence of the wheels' rumbling left a void which terrified him.

At last! The noise started up again in the distance. He glimpsed something red moving in the sky, behind the trees.

Then nothing.

Maigret stood utterly alone, clutching his shoulder with his right hand. It was his left shoulder that had been hit.

He tried to move his left arm and managed to raise it slightly, but it flopped back again, too heavy.

The woods were completely silent, suggesting that the man had not fled but was hiding in the undergrowth. If Maigret tried to reach the main road, might he not shoot again to finish him off?

'Idiot! Idiot! Idiot!' muttered Maigret, who felt utterly wretched.

Why had he felt the urge to jump off the train? At dawn his friend Leduc would be waiting for him at Villefranche station and his housekeeper would have cooked a salmon.

Maigret walked listlessly. He was forced to stop after three metres. He set off again, stopped once more.

Only the pale road stood out in the blackness, white and dusty like at the height of summer. Maigret was still bleeding, but not so profusely. His hand was stemming the flow and was covered in blood.

You would never have guessed that he had been wounded three times before. He was as scared as if on an operating table. He would prefer acute pain to this slow ebbing of blood.

It would be stupid to die here, tonight, all alone. Without even knowing where he was! While his luggage continued on its way without him!

'Too bad if the man shoots!' He walked as fast as he could, lurching forwards, feeling giddy. There was a signpost. But only the right hand side was lit up by a halo of moonlight: *3.5 km.*

What was at 3.5 km? Which town? Which village?

A cow mooed from that direction where the sky was a

little paler. That was probably the east. Dawn was about to break!

The stranger must have moved on. Or he had decided against trying to finish off the wounded inspector. Maigret calculated that he still had the strength to keep going for three or four minutes, and tried to make the most of it. He walked like a soldier, with regular steps, counting to stop himself from thinking.

The mooing cow must belong to a farm. Farmers rise early . . . Therefore—

The blood was seeping down his left side, beneath his shirt, beneath his trouser belt.

Was that a light he could see? Was he delirious already?

'If I lose more than a litre of blood—' he thought.

It was a light. But there was a ploughed field to cross and that was more difficult. His feet sank into the mud. He brushed past an abandoned tractor.

'Hello! . . . Someone! . . . Help! Quick!'

That desperate *quick* escaped him as he leaned against the tractor for support. He slid down and sat on the ground. He heard a door opening and made out a lantern swinging on the end of an arm.

'Quick!'

Hopefully the man who was coming over, getting closer, would be sharp-witted enough to staunch the bleeding! Meanwhile Maigret's hand lost its grip and fell limply to his side.

'One . . . two . . . one . . . two . . .'

The blood spurted out with every count.

★

Confused images, with blanks in between. All of them tinged with that note of panic that is the stuff of dreams.

A rhythm . . . The clip-clop of hooves . . . Straw under his head and trees filing past on his right.

That much, Maigret understood. He was lying in a cart. It was light. They were plodding slowly along a road lined with plane trees.

He opened his eyes without moving. Eventually a man entered his field of vision. He was sauntering along the road swinging a whip.

A nightmare? Maigret hadn't seen the face of the man from the train. All he knew of him was a vague form, patent-leather shoes and grey woollen socks.

So why did he think that the man leading the cart was the man from the train?

He saw a deeply lined face, with a bushy grey moustache and heavy eyebrows . . . and light-coloured eyes looking straight ahead, taking no notice of the wounded man.

Where were they? Where were they going?

Maigret's hand moved and he felt a strange wad around his chest, like a thick dressing.

Then his thoughts became muddled just as a ray of sunshine bored through his eyes into his brain.

Later there were houses, white façades . . . A wide street, bathed in light. Noise behind the cart, the noise of a crowd on the move . . . and voices . . . but he couldn't make out the words. The bumping made his wound hurt.

No more jolts . . . Just a swaying movement now, a rolling that he had never experienced before.

He was on a stretcher. In front of him was a man in a

white coat. A big gate clanged shut behind them and on the other side was a milling crowd. There was a sound of running footsteps.

'Take him to the operating theatre right away.'

He didn't move his head. He didn't think. But he looked.

They were crossing lawns dotted with small, pristine buildings. Men in grey uniforms sat on benches. Some had their heads or legs bandaged. Nurses were bustling about.

And in his sluggish mind, he tried, without success, to formulate the word 'hospital'.

Where was the farmer who looked like the man on the train? Ouch! They were going up some stairs. That hurt.

Maigret came to again to see a man washing his hands and looking at him gravely.

His heart skipped a beat. The man had a goatee, and busy eyebrows!

Did he look like the farmer? In any case, he looked like the man from the train!

Maigret couldn't speak. He opened his mouth. The man with the goatee said calmly, 'Put him in number three. It's best for him to be in isolation because of the police.'

Because of the police? What did he mean?

People in white transported him through the grounds again. The sunshine was brighter than any sunshine Maigret had ever seen – a sun so strong, so powerful, it seemed to reach the farthest recesses!

They were putting him in a bed. The walls were white. It was almost as hot as in the train. A voice was saying, 'It's the inspector who's asking when he'll be able to—'

The inspector – wasn't he the inspector? He hadn't asked

anything! This was ridiculous! Especially this business with the farmer who looked like the doctor and the man on the train!

But did the man on the train have a grey goatee? A moustache? Bushy eyebrows?

'Unclench his teeth . . . Good . . . Enough.'

The doctor was pouring something into his mouth.

To finish him off by poisoning him, of course!

When Maigret came round, towards evening, the nurse who was watching over him went out into the corridor where five men were waiting: the investigating magistrate from Bergerac, the prosecutor, the police inspector, a court clerk and the forensic pathologist.

'You may go in, but the doctor advises you not to tire him. He has such a strange look that I wouldn't be surprised if he's mad!'

And the five men exchanged knowing glances.